CW01597575

cycling with Margot

Nick Morrice

Illustrated by Harold Gosney

Q

isbn 978-1-912728-32-9

Published and printed by
Quacks Books
7 Grape Lane
Petergate
York YO1 7HU

Characters

Peter and Winnie - Run a smallholding in North Wales together with...

Henry - Sculptor and...

Don and Margot - Retired teacher and poet

Judith and Tammy - Writers in Derbyshire

Angus and Cynthia - Retired in Durham

James and David - Artists in Leeds

Phil and Rosie - Cycling tour operators in York

Cycling with Margot

The Lincolnshire Tales

Sitting at my desk with a cup of strong coffee to my right and a dark chocolate biscuit to my left, I feel I can begin. The problem has been that I don't write prose. Poetry has poured out of me all my life, but never prose, so this is taking a huge effort of will. But I'm having a somewhat better day than usual so at last I feel I can make a start.

Now I mustn't rush into this, like those books which seem to begin in the middle of something and you're supposed to work out who is who and what's going on almost as if you're clairvoyant. I can't be doing with that. Instead I will simply give you a little background information so that you know exactly where you are, and then we can "go forward", as they like to say nowadays, and continue the story.

Six years ago, my husband Don and I moved to North Wales to live with Winnie and Peter and Henry on Winnie's smallholding. If I'm completely honest I knew it wouldn't work out, at least for me. It was fine for Don, who likes lugging heavy gardening equipment around, and wielding axes and suchlike, but you see I'm not really a country girl. Like A E Housman, who never set foot in Shropshire as far as I'm aware, I like the idea of the countryside and I write about the countryside, but actually to live in it has never been my idea of heaven.

However, Don was besotted with the notion of moving there so I went along with it. I know what it's like to have obsessions and there's no escape from them, so I dutifully, and with a great show of enthusiasm, complied. And there was much to enjoy too. The best thing was getting to know Marcie and Isabel, Winnie's lovely girls. Marcie reminded me of Hardy's Tess - a beautiful but slightly vulnerable child of nature - and Isabel, her older and stronger sister, who was so protective of her. I loved watching the two of them together, and grew very fond of them.

But I couldn't settle down. I tried hard and everybody was very sweet to me, but it was no good. The locals did their best to make me feel at home, and the countryside was certainly beautiful in its wild and rugged way. But there wasn't a café for miles – no shops, no library, no cinema, no restaurants. I was having serious withdrawal symptoms, and I needed more noise, and bus routes, and roads and pavements. Ridiculous, really, but there it was. I am a towny through and through, and I was going into meltdown.

Above all, I missed Rosie, Phil's lovely wife who I had grown so fond of since our cycling holidays had begun. The internet was hopeless in North Wales so I was stuck with writing endlessly long letters to Rosie and then waiting about a week for a reply, which was very frustrating. Rosie and Phil lived in York and I began to realise I needed to be near them. I also needed a community of like-minded people where I could join book groups, and writing circles, and go to concerts and have long earnest conversations over coffee in lovely warm cafés. But all I had for company here whenever I left the house were herds of bleating sheep!

I used to pour out my feelings to Rosie, and one day a letter came back from her telling me about a retirement community which I might be interested in. It was about three miles from the centre of York and had been built by the Joseph Rowntree Housing Trust twenty or so years ago as a Continuing Care Retirement Community for older people in the UK.

I immediately got on the phone to her, and she told me more.

"The development consists of 150 one or two bedroom bungalows, and it has a Care Centre, which has over 40 rooms. There are also extensive communal facilities – a restaurant, a coffee shop, an arts and crafts room, a library, a music room, a shop, a hydrotherapy pool and a small fitness centre..."

Can you believe how excited I was!

"Give me their phone number, Rosie. I'm going to ring them right away."

Within a week Don and I were walking into the reception area, and immediately I knew I had come home. It was like walking into a hotel, for there behind the desk was an elegant lady who greeted us with a beaming smile - and the smell of strong coffee hung in the air - and there was a table covered in magazines with lovely soft armchairs - and it was warm! It was then I realised that for the last few years I had been shivering with cold in North Wales, and now I was feeling warm again.

"This is it, Don. We're going to come and live here for the rest of our lives."

"But you haven't even seen inside the bungalow yet, and anyway I'm not sure we'll be able to afford it."

"Just forget all that. I mean to come here, and no argument."

The first thing to do was tell the others, which was a bit sad, especially for the girls who became quite tearful. I did explain that it would probably take a year or two before we moved as there was a long waiting list, and then we had to go to Open Days, and be approved on medical grounds and take some sort of mental test, which sounded alarming. (Later on this turned out to be nothing more than identifying a paper clip and knowing that I wasn't Queen of England.)

But we did apply, and went through all the procedures patiently - and after a year we were settled in our own little chalet bungalow, with our own tiny garden, lovely neighbours, on a good bus route to central York, and a flat cycle path into the city. And above all a community of friendly people all of whom lived within a hundred yards of my very own front door. Bliss!

So that is how Don and I came to live so close to the most wonderful city in England. York! I thought Exeter was heaven on earth, but York - with all its Roman and Viking history, medieval walls, fabulous Minster, Georgian architecture, glorious library and art gallery, markets and shops, festivals, street entertainers, concerts, theatres, a wonderful art cinema, and more cafés and restaurants than you could possibly visit in a whole lifetime - is even better.

And now I could spend hours and hours of time with Rosie!

This all happened about two years ago when Don and I were 65 (he said at the time that he was far too young to move to a retirement community but I pointed out that 65 was a perfectly respectable age at which to retire and surely he was retired anyway?). We immediately threw ourselves into the community and in a strange way began leading separate lives. He started doing things like ping-pong (sorry, the Table Tennis Group - they were snooty about that) and helping with gardening in the grounds and joining the Residents Committee and going on long cycle rides with Geoffrey and Martin, so really he was quite happy without me. I, on the other hand, joined an International Group which gave talks about countries I had barely even heard of - and I started doing weaving! I went to the Art Group although I knew nothing about painting or drawing, and I got roped into joining the Hanging Committee, which is not as gruesome as it sounds. So in these and various other ways we gradually came to know all the interesting people who lived in our community.

There was no Writers' Group, however, so I felt it was my duty to set one up. I did some research and came across a young teacher from York called Gary, who would come and facilitate it. We would have to pay him, of course, but I found four residents who were prepared to pay a modest sum, and so a brand new Writers' Group was formed. I felt so proud! We consisted of two men, Justin and Alfred, and two ladies, Isabel and Frances, and myself. Justin was tall and thin, with a soft voice and serious expression. Alfred was short and round, quite loud and always laughing and cracking jokes. Isabel was elegance personified with a somewhat lofty manner but a sweet temper, while Frances was dour, grim-faced and blunt.

Gary turned out to be a breath of fresh air. At our first group meeting, we did some ice-breaking games.

"I want you to walk around the room and greet each other, first in a shy and reserved manner, but as you proceed, with an ever-increasing level of confidence." By the end we were going overboard: "HALLOOOO!! How lovely to meet you, darling!" and it was really quite funny.

Next we had to speak to a partner for fifty seconds on any subject we liked, which was surprisingly difficult but a good way of loosening up. Then we struck a heroic pose, which I can't say worked very well, as none of us looked in the least bit heroic. We were better at the final game called, "Oi, get out of my pub", although Isabel was altogether too refined for this and never quite managed the rough cockney manner. "I need to watch more episodes of *Eastenders*, probably," she said, but I don't expect she ever will.

At last it was time to settle down and do some writing.

"Try your hand at updating a nursery rhyme," said Gary. We were given five minutes of writing time, and then we went round the room reciting them. I enjoyed Frances' best:

Sing a song of sixpence,
A pocket full of rye.
Ouch! get off my foot
Or I'll squirt you in the eye!

Which shows the sort of person she was.

The second exercise was to take the point of view of a secondary character in a pantomime, and Justin chose to be an Ugly Sister from *Cinderella*:

I know I'm not a looker
(And my sister's no great shakes)
But to label me as ugly -
What a mean and cruel mistake!
I confess I am not dainty
Which is why I lost the prize,
That bloomin' little slipper's
Far too small for my foot size.

Again, pretty clever for ten minutes' work.

Next was a real mind-stretcher. We had to imagine we were children, sitting in the back of the classroom with a spare seat next to us. An object from the natural world comes and sits beside us, and we engage in conversation. It was suggested we might like to write this in free verse. Isabel came up with the best:

On a warm dreamy afternoon -
It is History Revision -
I hear this lapping of water
And a desert island washes up beside me,
Complete with foam-flecked shore line
And swaying palm trees.
"Come on board," she murmurs enticingly
So I curl the warm grains of sand

Between my fingers and toes
And roll up the beach.
History, of course, became a thing of the past.

Brilliant, although Isabel dismissed it as 'a mere whimsy.'

The final exercise was the most challenging. We had to write about someone famous, but keep their name until the very last moment, when we would stop - and hope the others guessed it. Alfred, who was the best at rhyming, wrote a brilliant one:

Hair on end, chubby face,
Shirt hangs out all over the place,
Teeth stick out, goofy grin,
Rosy cheeks, wobbly chin,
Cheeky smile, ever joking,
Ribs a-tickling and a-poking,
Funny man, queer and odd
But what a performer! ....

And we all shouted, "Ken Dodd!"

Now what might all this have to do with cycling, you might reasonably ask. We had not done one of our cycling holidays for ages, because we were all so far flung, and some of us were busy with work and so on. But all that had been changing in recent years. For instance, Angus and Cynthia were now happily settled in Durham, James and David had moved to Leeds, both with arty kind of jobs, while Judith and Tammy had moved to Derbyshire to be nearer Tammy's parents. Phil, Rosie, Don and I were all in York, so the only 'far-flung' people were Winnie, Peter and Henry.

Another point was (and I am going to mention this as quickly as possible, after which the subject is taboo) I had been given a diagnosis which signalled something like, "Come in, number 17, your time's up." There, enough said.

So there was every good reason to organise one final cycling holiday. I also had an idea which had sprung from the Writers' Group. Don and I worked out a route which we thought would take about a week to cycle, and then it was simply a matter of informing everyone. This is the email I wrote that night:

Dear friends and fellow cyclists, the dearest of my heart,
It's been too many years that we have been apart.
It's time we reunited, joined hands and hugged and kissed
Slipped on the clips, the helmets, and cycled through the mist.

From York to Market Weighton, to Beverley and Hull,
Across the bridge to Lincolnshire - and never say it's dull!
Some hidden gems await us like a medieval maze,
And lovely rolling countryside to brighten up our days.

Now here's an extra challenge - it's all part of my scheme -
To write an artful poem on some topic, or a theme
Which inspires in you a passion, a burning revelation,
And these we'll read as we proceed, for fun and relaxation.

Don't worry about quality - simple doggerel will do
Which tells a tale of wonderment or deeds of derring-do,
A ballad or a song perhaps, of mystery and might,
Whatever you can muster will provide us with delight.

Over the next couple of days everyone replied, and here is what they wrote:

"*The Lincolnshire Tales* - we love it! Keep us informed. Judith and Tammy."

"Dear Margot, Brilliant! We'll be there. Angus and Cynthia."

"High time someone organised this. Great! And we can make use of David's house in Beverley. James and David."

(I should explain that David's parents has died tragically a year ago, so the house now belonged to him.)

"Yes, please! Need help with the bookings? Phil and Rosie."

"We need a break, so thanks a million. Peter and Winnie."

But a somewhat dubious note was sounded by Henry: "Oh dear, not Lincolnshire - but I must face up to it one day, I suppose. Yes, I'll be there - H." Very mysterious.

We took Rosie and Phil up on their offer of sorting out the final details, and met them a few days later at our favourite café in town.

"Rosie has a way of knowing what's best," said Phil, "and she has already made a good start."

"I think we should meet for breakfast at the Station Hotel in York on the first day, and set off from there," she said.

We agreed.

"Go on, Rosie."

"The first day will be the longest ride, and will take us east to Stamford Bridge, then Pocklington, where we can have our first break. We'll continue east to Market Weighton, then to Beverley and all that comes to about 43 miles. Beverley is a lovely town, and we can spend a night there."

"Sounds good so far."

"Day Two will be much lighter. We go south across the Humber Bridge into Lincolnshire, then cycle south-east to visit Thornton Abbey and Gatehouse. It's an English Heritage property and is open every day from 10.00 o'clock so we can stop for a visit. There is a large Bed and Breakfast place in Barnetby le Wold, which will be able to accommodate us all. Then on to Caistor, an old Roman town on the north edge of the Wolds."

"Isn't she brilliant?" said Phil proudly, and we had to agree.

"From there it's less than 30 miles to Lincoln, but we could have a break at Market Rasen, which is a little under half way, before cycling along some country lanes into the city."

"I would like to spend two nights in Lincoln," I said. "There's plenty to see there, I'm sure, apart from the cathedral."

"Oh yes, we must spend two nights there. But there won't be much time for sightseeing," said Rosie.

"Why do you say that?"

"I have a feeling there'll be something else to do when we arrive, but I'm not sure exactly what it is yet."

"What are you talking about?"

"It's something to do with Henry which we don't yet know but was suggested by his email. It will come out on this trip, and then we'll have to do something to help him. I'm sorry to sound so vague and mysterious. But Henry is the thirteenth member of the group, and he's the only one who's unattached. So there is something not quite right there, and it needs to be resolved. There's obviously some issue in his past he needs to come to terms with, and that's what we're going to be helping him with."

"Rosie is having one of her hunches," said Phil, winking at us, "so we must humour her, mustn't we, love?"

"I might well be wrong. Anyway, after that we are going to visit Phil's mum in Winterton, which is a sweet little village in north Lincolnshire. She's a funny old thing, but quite wise in her way. Phil has friends and relations there who will put us up, and they will take us to Julian's Bower in Alkborough, which is a medieval grass maze."

Don and I exchanged glances of curiosity, but Rosie carried on regardless.

"After Winterton we head back across the Humber Bridge, then cycle west towards Howden, Selby and finally the Solar System route to York."

"Solar system?"

"Yes. There are scale models of the planets all along the Selby to York cycle route, but the track itself which used to be a railway line is also a wonderful nature reserve. So that's it - how does it sound?"

We thought it sounded perfect - and I felt a frisson of excitement at the thought of unravelling the mystery of Henry.

And on that slightly tantalising note, we left Phil and Rosie to sort out all the finer details.

Cycling Trip: Friday

Don and I found ourselves cycling in the semi-darkness of an August morning across the meadows towards York Station. It reminded me of my childhood summer holidays when we would be up at 5:00 am, and after a bowl of Cornflakes, steal out of the house barely whispering to each other so as not to disturb the neighbours, load up the car and drive away like guilty creatures creeping noiselessly through the night.

There was a cool mist suspended over the fields. A half moon was setting in the west, and the first streaks of a rosy dawn were spreading across the eastern sky. The damp smell of haymaking was hanging in the air, which was moist on our faces from the night's rainfall. The burning heat of July was over and we could look forward to milder temperatures for the journey ahead.

We arrived far too early but fortunately the cafés at York station were open, so we lingered over a coffee and read our books until we felt we could decently make our appearance at the hotel. Occasionally Don would go out and take a look around the platforms, because we knew James and David would have caught an early train from Leeds, as well as Angus and Cynthia coming from Durham. Others making longer journeys would probably have booked into the hotel the previous night.

I was beginning to fall asleep when I felt my shoulder being shaken.

"Wake up, Margot, look who's arrived!"

"David! James! You're so tanned! Where have you been?"

James was wearing pale blue shorts, trainers and a yellow T-shirt, and his familiar blue eyes were sparkling out of a dark unshaven face. He gave me a big hug and explained,

"We have been in Crete for two weeks, lolling on the beaches and by the hotel pool. These are the results!"

My memory of David was as a pasty-faced, undernourished young man, but now he looked the picture of health and energy. With a few years' teaching behind him, he seemed totally transformed - tall, upright, confident, with a beaming face 'like a prophet new inspired', as Angus might have quoted. Even his hug was strong and firm, not like the weak limp thing I remembered. In his cream-coloured jeans and striped pink shirt, he was no longer the pale shadow of James and he also had more to say for himself.

"We haven't been totally lazy. I've never swum so much in my life," he said. "Actually it was a totally free holiday for us. A friend of our agent had put us in touch with a Greek tourist agency which was bringing out a new line in 'Islands of the Aegean' travel books, all with original paintings as opposed to photographs. They had seen our work in the 'Coloured Counties' series, liked it and gave us the contract for Crete. And my pal here," giving James a quick nudge, "is so quick nowadays that a couple of hours work a day, and he's knocked off another landscape."

"Anyway, we want to hear about you. Tell us about this new community you're living in," said James.

We became so engrossed in our conversation that I wasn't aware of Cynthia and Angus until I felt the warm gentle touch of a hand on my shoulder. I looked up and there was Cynthia's smiling face looking down into mine.

"Hello, dear cycling friends!"

We quickly found two more chairs and had soon settled into some more catching up. Cynthia was wearing strawberry-coloured trousers in light flowing cotton. She was as thin as ever, but looked tanned and healthy, and her grey hair, now silvering beautifully, was swept back into a tight bun to reveal her radiant face and blue-grey eyes. She looked as calm and self-possessed as ever. Angus, short and stocky, his hair still jet black, cheeks and lips full and ruddy, wore his usual serious expression with furrowed brow. But it only took a joke from James for his face to break into a wide grin and he then reminded me of some Green Man of the Woods.

"Well met, everyone, for our next instalment."('Well met' was a favourite greeting of his - any excuse to introduce a touch of Shakespeare.) "And well done, Margot, for organising us, stirring us into action."

I had always been in awe of Cynthia and Angus, whom I would call ascetic and disciplined - and therefore quite unlike me. For example, they never drank alcohol, and while Angus allowed himself tea 'for fortifying purposes', Cynthia only ever drank hot water. With their wills of iron and intense manner of speech, they were a daunting couple, and somehow seemed to set a high standard which the rest of us could only aspire to.

It was eight o'clock by now so it was time to make our way to breakfast. We wheeled our bikes into the station forecourt, through the taxi rank and incoming tide of people, out into the sunshine and the early morning melée of buses and cars. The day promised well with a cloudless sky and only a light wind.

Now I'm aware I mustn't linger long over this preamble so I will skirt over the pleasurable details of our reunion.

Looking back, I suppose the conversation with Winnie and Peter over breakfast proved significant in terms of how the week unfolded. They were both looking quite tired and much older than I'd expected, and must have been looking forward to a holiday from the endless round of work which faced them on a daily basis at their smallholding.

"We know we can't stay there forever, mainly because it is too big for us now that the girls have left home, and also the workload is wearisome nowadays," said Winnie. "But the problem is, what to do about Henry? He has never once referred to any family so we can only assume he doesn't have one, or he's lost touch with whatever he did have."

"Have you ever asked him?"

"Only once, and he clammed up at once, so it was obviously a subject he didn't want to talk about."

"The only hint we've ever had about his past," said Peter, "was when you sent out the email about this cycling holiday. It really shook him, but we've no idea why."

I told them about his mysterious reply.

"I'd always assumed he came from Edinburgh," said Don, "although I admit he doesn't have a Scottish accent."

"He's been much quieter over the past few weeks," said Winnie. "I think he might be preparing himself to face up to something, but I'm only guessing. Most of the time he's been as cheerful as ever, throwing himself into all the work of the farm, seemingly tireless, almost manic at times. But the more immediate question is, what are we going to do with him if we sell up?"

"Have you got some new idea?"

Peter and Winnie looked at each other, and smiled.

"Go on, you tell them," said Peter.

"All right," said Winnie, putting down her knife and fork. "Our dream would be to run a Bed and Breakfast place, in some attractive rural location..."

"...with a good size garden, a few chickens, a couple of dogs...", went on Peter.

"...and a cat. And I could carry on making jams and chutney..."

"... and I could go to a nearby pub and have chats with the locals..."

"...and we would still have a home for the girls to come back to..."

"...and it would be somewhere in Yorkshire, not too far from you two!" concluded Peter.

"Oh, wouldn't that be wonderful, Don!" I exclaimed, and he was clearly as delighted at the prospect as I was.

"But you see our problem."

"Yes, because you wouldn't particularly want to take Henry with you."

And Don added, "Or want to abandon him."

We all fell silent, while the waitress topped up our coffee and offered us more toast. Then Phil and Rosie approached our table.

"What are you four looking so thoughtful about?" asked Phil.

Very briefly Winnie explained the situation.

"Henry's been sitting with us," said Rosie, "and he struck me as unusually quiet. Something seems to be on his mind, but there's no telling what."

"Rosie will get to the bottom of it," said Phil confidently. "She always does, you know."

"I wouldn't say that," replied Rosie, "but I will have a quiet word with him and remind him we're all the best of friends, and if he has anything he wants to talk about, then this week might be a good time to get it off his chest. I'll try and help him if I possibly can. He's such a dear man."

If anyone could help, then Rosie would find a way so we left it at that. Others were getting up from their tables, so it was nearly time to be on our way.

We set off on the old railway line, now a cycle track, in the direction of Osbaldwick village and Dunnington. The day had turned dull, drizzly and cold so it was difficult to feel inspired. The countryside beyond York had that tired look of late summer. At the edges of fields a few red poppies were clinging to life but didn't exactly fill one with joy, nor did half a dozen damp-looking llamas near Limehouse Farm. Rutted tracks were filling with water making it difficult to steer a straight line. Swifts were flying around as lively as ever, presaging the beginning of autumn, and the rain was already starting to creep under my collar. By 11:00 o'clock we had arrived, dripping wet, in Pocklington and were ready for a break.

"I think we should split up," announced Phil, "so we don't all impose ourselves on one café."

This seemed a good idea, so Winnie, Judith, Tammy and I set off as a group. We found an appealing little delicatessen, where we ordered our drinks and scones at the counter, and were told to find a table upstairs.

"Don't worry about the drips, dear," the kindly waitress replied to my apologetic remarks. "Make yourselves comfy and we'll bring your order up in a few minutes."

Upstairs were three small connected rooms which offered a haven of peace and calm. Under dark oak beams two elderly gentlemen were sitting in silence at polished oak tables reading their newspapers, while in a quiet corner a young mother with a babe in arms was talking in hushed tones to a lady who I guessed to be her mother. A black leather sofa was taken over by a man and his OS map, and that left one table for us. Carefully removing our sodden garments and hanging them on the backs of the chairs we started to feel human again.

"I don't know how you do it," I said to Tammy, as I watched her remove her helmet, allowing her long auburn hair to fall elegantly round her perfectly made-up face, looking as though she had arrived at a dinner party. "We look as though we've narrowly escaped drowning while you look like a serene swan."

Tammy laughed.

"Actually I loved the morning ride, with its flat landscape and the wide open views across fields. We don't have anything like that near us."

I asked Judith about her blossoming writing career.

"To be honest, I seem to have hit a dry spot. I have tried a few ideas but nothing seems to be working out very well. I am looking for a good story - maybe something will turn up over the next few days."

We lingered over our coffee as long as we could in the comfort and warmth but thirty minutes was the time limit so we reluctantly put on our wet things, thanked the staff and set off into the rain which showed no sign of letting up.

The next stop was Market Weighton, but I noticed that my electric bike battery was discharging rapidly and I would definitely need to top it up somewhere. Fortunately the public library was open so I decided to call in there, while everyone else saw what there was to see in the town. But I thought I'd better ask first.

"Excuse me, but please may I plug this in?" and I explained what I was after.

"I will go and ask," the young lady replied, and in a few moments the manager appeared from one of the back rooms.

"I'm afraid it's out of the question. You see, all our equipment here is PAT tested, and it would be against Health and Safety regulations to let you recharge your bike battery."

I could hardly believe what I was hearing but, trying to be as polite and calm as possible, I asked whether she could make any other suggestions in view of the distance I still had to travel and the appalling weather conditions. She um'd and er'd a good deal, and eventually took pity on me.

"But you must stay with the battery at all times."

"Oh, I promise I won't let it out of my sight."

"How long do you think it will take?"

"Only about half an hour, I should think."

"I suggest you use this little corner," she said, indicating the children's section and a low plastic chair which I could sit on.

"Thank you, I'm very much obliged," I said with feeling. I was quite looking forward to my rest but was soon interrupted by Henry who it seemed was also seeking a break from the rain. On seeing me squatting among a small pile of picture books, he approached and said,

"Margot, I'm having serious problems with my poem - you know, my Lincolnshire Tale. I don't remember ever writing a poem before and I'm really struggling with the rhymes and the rhythm. Would you mind taking a look at the few verses I've done so far?"

He called it "Confessions of a Lad from Lincolnshire", and it was clearly going to be a revelatory poem about his past life. I shan't quote any of it here for the obvious reason that you will hear it in its entirety later. I was able to help tidy it up so that by the time my battery was charged it was sounding better and Henry knew how to carry on.

"That's wonderful!" he exclaimed. "Perhaps I could come to you again if I hit a problem."

"Of course," I replied, and was about to ask him whether he was totally happy about the subject matter, when the rest of the party started appearing in the library, eager to make a move.

"You missed the sculpture of the Giant," said one, and then another, and then another. By the time eight different photographs of the Market Weighton Giant were shown to me, I felt fully satisfied I had seen it.

"Anyway, I've been enjoying Henry's company. We've been discussing iambic verse and patterns of rhyme."

Before leaving, I knocked on the door of the library manager's office and expressed my profuse thanks for her kindness.

"You really have saved my life," I said.

She gave me a sweet smile and said, "Not at all!" We parted the best of friends.

The next question was where to stop for lunch, which was not a great prospect. We had all come with sandwiches and the rain was pouring down more heavily than ever.

"Hopefully we will find a shelter somewhere," said Peter usefully.

"Look!" exclaimed Don. "There's a bus shelter over there."

"Don't be ridiculous!" I said. "I'm sure if we head out of town we'll find a dry barn somewhere. Come on, follow me. Route 66, isn't it?"

I don't know what possessed me to be so assertive, but fortune favours the brave and I led the way out of town for about half a mile until, on the left-hand side of the road, appeared a huge dry barn with plenty of straw bales. It provided the perfect shelter from the rain.

It was while we were settling down for our picnic that I thought it was time for the first of our "Lincolnshire Tales."

"James, are you ready with your poem?"

"Yes, I am. I'd asked Margot if I could go first - then I can relax." So we sat down at his feet munching our crisps while he gave us a short preamble.

"I don't know much about poetry, but when I was in New Zealand at my sister's wedding in the Coromandel Peninsula, I remembered a poem by Edward Lear, so this is inspired by him. It becomes rather sad and reflective towards the end - I don't know why."

"Just before you start," I said, "I have, in true Chaucerian fashion, written little introductions for everyone. Here is yours, James, and then you can begin."

Young James spoke first, an artist strong and bold,
Whose fame is spreading far and wide (we're told).
The RA talent-scouts have not yet heard
About his brushwork, so we'll spread the word.
Those hallowed walls his paintings will adorn,
Then membership is his, and all will fawn.

"I certainly won't become famous for my poetry, so thank you for your encouraging lines, Margot. In case you haven't heard of it, the Pohutakawa is the iconic Kiwi Christmas tree."

The Song of Coromandel

On the shores of Coromandel
Where the Norfolk Island Pines
Stand tall and proud as the waves crash loud
And the sun in the west declines,
I saw two children playing
And a dog barked at their fun,
They heedless were of the passing hours
And the setting of the sun.

On the shores of Coromandel
Where Pohutakawa grows
I met a man with a camper van
And asked him where he goes.
"I go to Whangapoua
Where the waves crash on the beach,
And there bewail my lost sweetheart,
Forever beyond my reach.

"The waves of Whangapoua
Are white with crested foam
Like hedgerows in the wintertime
When fringed with falls of snow.
They rear and rise before me.
I breathe in deep to face
The tumbling swirling freedom
Of their watery embrace."

On the shores of Coromandel
Where the fine Karaka glows
With glossy leaves and orange seeds
The silver moon arose.
Its gentle beams cast cooling light
Upon the sandy shore,
And still the waves crashed long and loud
As they will for ever more.

And so my life befalls me
When prospects, heavy-laid
With possible disaster
And fear and doom, will fade
Into a gentle river
Of rippling events,
And I'm left breathless, laughing,
Reckless of the expense.

There was a round of applause from everyone and Judith asked for the last verse to be read again which James did. On that thoughtful note we proceeded on our wet and dreary way (oh dear, what a shame to be writing this!) because from then on the rain got heavier and heavier and the remainder of the ride to Beverley was one of unmitigated discomfort and misery. (I exaggerate really but I don't think I have ever been wetter.)

As I said earlier, David now owned the family home in Beverley, following the tragic deaths of his parents. It was looked after by a housekeeper until such time as he decided whether or not to sell it. It had been arranged that Don and I would stay with James and David, so they took us there while everyone else found their prearranged accommodation in the town. The housekeeper, Miriam, had offered to arrange dinner for us all, which I thought was very handsome of her.

"I'll see to all your wet things - there is plenty of drying space here. David, show them to their rooms, they're all ready for you - and there's plenty of hot water for showers."

There were also thick fluffy towels and full-length white bathrobes, and within half an hour, wearing our spare set of clothes which fortunately had kept dry in the panniers, we were sipping tea and eating digestive biscuits in the comfort of David's spacious living room. Talk about elegant living! With its French windows opening out onto a well-maintained garden with manicured lawns and colourful flower beds, I could well understand David's reluctance to sell his family home.

Now I am conscious that I must move the story on, so I will skip over the gradual arrival of the party, and the delicious fish pie supper followed by strawberry cake that Miriam had cooked for us. I've never cooked for thirteen people in my life, and I wouldn't know where to start. Anyway it was wonderful, and Don made a little speech which Miriam appreciated. After dinner there was time to relax and listen to the next poem. David as host decided to say his.

"I wrote this many years ago, during my gap year when I did some travelling in India and Nepal. I worked at a school in Kathmandu for a while and admired the kids for their cheerfulness even when they were obviously so poor. There were four in particular, two boys and two girls, whose stories really touched me. It seemed that nobody had ever told them stories or read them poems, so I decided to write one myself."

"First, here's your introduction," I said.

James' partner, David, quiet, modest, shy,
Prefers to keep his skills from public eye,
But what unerring taste and - pardon my cheek! -
Where James has flash and flair, David's technique
May better pass that crucial test of time...
Comparisons be gone! Best end my rhyme.

"Flash and flair, eh?" said James. "Hmm, not sure I like that."

"Shh! I'm only kidding," I said, and David began:

The Ballad of Kathmandu

This is a tale from far Nepal where once two sisters dwelt,
Their childhood was perfect, such love and peace they felt
From their parents who adored them, had brought them up by hand,
Their mother did the cooking, their father tilled the land.

Saraswati, the firstborn, with a name so divine:
Knowledge, music, art and grace - she bore every sign
Of displaying special talents from her early childhood years,
Endowed with a sweet temper, never shedding tears.

Her sister's name, Sapana, in Nepalese means "Dream",
By her teachers and her relatives was held in high esteem
For her sense of fun, adventure and carefree way of living,
Always friendly and affectionate, always happy to be giving.

Next door there lived two brothers, Ashish the elder's name.
He loved to sing and dance, and hoped to rise to fame.
Brijesh, the younger quieter one, wrote songs of peace and love -
With his guitar he sang at night to the stars in heaven above.

When they left school, their every hope was focused on Kathmandu.
"Let's break into the music scene with something fresh and new.
Come with us, Saraswati, and Sapana, come as well.
We'll form a group, and with our songs we'll weave a magic spell."

Immediately Sapana said, "We're excited beyond measure.
To join your group is bliss for us, beyond every known pleasure."
"That surely is the perfect name: 'Beyond' - don't you agree?"
Said Brijesh, and all concurred with him: it suited perfectly.

Their parents gave a blessing to the youngsters' enterprise.
"Good luck, and with your talents we are sure you'll win a prize
For creating songs of beauty, songs of peace and love and joy.
With your music touch the hearts of every girl and every boy."

They said farewell to uncles, aunts, their parents and their pets –
A few shed tears, of course, but there were really no regrets.
They gathered their belongings and climbed aboard a bus,
Saraswati saying simply, "Please pray and think of us."

Many villages they passed through, forests, meadows, mountain streams
Until at last they came in sight of the city of their dreams.
It shone below them radiantly in the light of the midday sun,
The spires of temples whispering, "Come and join the fun!"

A friendly man gave good advice in answering their questions.
"Sing your songs in Ratna Park - I'll give you the directions."
The four musicians hurried on. What crowded, dusty places!
How stressed and tired the people looked! So many careworn faces!

"I hope our songs will bring some change," said Sapana with a sigh.
Ashish replied, "They'll bring delight to every passer-by!"
"Let's change into some coloured clothes," suggested Saraswati,
"A hippie image will make our show more chic - more like a party!"

So on the way to Ratna Park they bought in quick succession
Headbands, bracelets, flares and tops - a colourful impression
They'd make upon their audience, to give them more delight.
Their performances would be enhanced - a feast of sound and sight!

When they arrived, they looked around - soon found a shaded spot
Where people sat enjoying a chat, and the sun was not too hot.
The girls warmed up their voices, the boys strummed their guitars -
They launched into their first song, "Welcome to the stars!"

Kids stopped playing on the swings, mothers ceased their chatter,
Men looked up as if to say, "What is all the matter?"
And soon they were excited by this new sound from 'Beyond',
Songs so beautiful and sweet for which they all had longed.

Saraswati and Sapana in their colourful array
Touched the hearts of everyone on that afternoon in May.
Ashish and Brijesh played their guitars in pleasant harmony
Adding colour and enrichment to the glorious melody.

After twenty minutes singing the group began to move
With a kind of steady purpose: they had a point to prove.
The audience followed after them, captured by the spell
Of such enchanting music which would all cares dispel.

Out into the busy roads, not thinking of their lives,
Their only thought to reach the goal from which their name derives,
Beyond the cares and troubles which they saw in many a face,
They'd find the one true joy - and put that in its place.

They sang around the temples, they strummed around the shrines,
Everywhere they went they captivated hearts and minds.
When they arrived at Durbar Square, some steep steps they ascended
And gazed down at the vast crowd which upon them now attended.

Ashish spoke thus: "My dearest friends, we've come from distant parts
Hoping with our music to soothe any troubled hearts.
We strive for compositions with melodies sublime
And words which are appealing beyond all space and time.

"Once more we'll sing our repertoire, then on our way we'll go.
Please use your phones to film us, and immortalise our show.
Maybe we'll get on YouTube for all the world to see
How music can transform the lives of you – and you – and me!"

Again they played and sang their songs, and lifted many a load.
The people showered them with cash: "Now take it on the road.
Travel far beyond the city, to east and west Nepal,
They need to hear this music, so perform it for them all."

'Beyond' that day left Kathmandu, but their memory lingers on:
Their coloured clothes, headbands and rings, guitars and soothing song.
They lifted all who heard them from sadness, frets and fears,
Imparting youthful feelings, wiping away life's tears.

It's said they travelled o'er a year, beyond all expectations,
Returning home at last to their friends and their relations.
The group decided to disband: "All things must come to pass,
But our friendship is forever - no beyond! That will last!"

We responded with an enthusiastic round of applause, and then I asked David if the children understood the poem.

"Their English was surprisingly good but a lot of the vocabulary was new to them, so it was a chance to teach them some new words. It's a lovely country but has all sorts of social and economic problems. Even now I believe it's one of the poorest countries in the world, and life there is very tough."

Hoping for better weather tomorrow, we said goodnight and made our way to our various beds.

Saturday

We met at the Market Cross in Beverley at 9:00 o'clock. Everything had dried out overnight so we were raring to go. The day looked much better - windy and sunny, with the clouds high in the sky.

It took us nearly an hour and half to arrive at the Humber Bridge, where we saw a sign saying, *Runners are currently taking part in a long distance endurance race which may last anywhere between six and thirty-six hours and they are likely to be emotional. Please resist the urge to feed them, pet them, or feel sorry for them. They chose to do this.* There were some tents nearby, perhaps belonging to friends and family who would be giving the runners emotional support, poor things.

It was no great surprise to encounter much puffing and panting as we sped past runners of all shapes and sizes. Fabulous views of the river, and it was exciting to see Lincolnshire ahead. Do people normally get excited about entering Lincolnshire? Probably not, but we were very excited on that breezy Saturday morning as we cycled into the sunshine. After the appalling miseries of the day before, we felt that the holiday proper was about to start.

Barton on Humber - quaint, a bit seedy, old-fashioned but rather charming in a down-at-heel kind of way. Soon we were out into the countryside through fields of ripening corn, bright gold in the morning sun, puffy white clouds drifting across the sky, hedges of hawthorn bright with ripening berries, pigeons and rooks blown by the wind.

Eventually we arrived at Thornton Abbey gatehouse, an extraordinary relic now preserved by English Heritage. A sign read, *This is the largest monastic gatehouse in England; architectural symbol of wealth and power from the late Middle Ages.* Fascinating to see the old stone sculptures on the façade, and the wooden doorways in a state of crumbling deterioration, quaint and evocative.

Nearby in a field a farmer had created a maze in his field of sweetcorn, and a large sign, next to a vast red pumpkin perched on a tree trunk with a face carved out as if for Halloween, stated **Maize Maze.**

"Now that gives me an idea," said Judith excitedly. "Didn't somebody say that we were going to visit another maze later in the week?"

"Yes, that's right," said Rosie. "It's at a place called Alkborough, east of here and a few miles north of Scunthorpe."

"Good. I can make use of this," remarked Judith rather mysteriously.

By now a large black rain cloud had appeared out of nowhere and within five minutes we were cycling through a heavy downpour. It was going to be one of those "showers with sunny intervals" kind of days, and by the time we reached the Thornton Hunt Inn at Thornton

Cross, we had received a soaking but almost dried out again.

Now here was a pub which time had passed by. Most pubs nowadays seem to offer fancy sophisticated menus at high prices, but here you could buy beer and a cheese sandwich for only a few pounds. Also it was quiet with no piped music. A local came and chatted to us about where we'd been and where we were going.

"Oh, Barnetby le Wold, you say. Some funny folk there. Make sure you lock up your bikes carefully. I won't say any more."

It wasn't perhaps the cheeriest of conversations, but at least he had showed an interest in us.

"Can I read my poem now?" asked Tammy. We looked towards the local who nodded approvingly, so Tammy carried on.

"You all know the Angel of the North, the sculpture by Antony Gormley, which stands on a hill near Gateshead overlooking the A1. In 1998 it celebrated its twentieth anniversary, so I decided to write a poem about it."

"But first...," and I said my little piece:

A lady spoke whose elegance and charm
And beauty, grace and wit could all disarm.
If any, like us, may once become her friend
Then joy alone prevails - all sorrows end.
I speak of Tammy who blogs in prose sublime
And touches readers' heartstrings every time.

"Thank you, Margot. Here goes."

The Song of the Angel of the North

I dreamt I saw an angel watching from above
Yorkshire's shining county with a look of care and love:
"I bless your purple moorlands, your forests and your hills,
From the mighty Ouse and Humber to the smallest trickling rills."

He began his flight of blessing in the western rolling dales
Where Ingleborough and Penyghent look down on verdant vales,
The great whaleback of Whernside crouching like a beast
And Mickle Fell, the highest of this quartet of peaks.

His airy way pursuing over Buttertubs Pass,
Adorned with fragrant primroses, thyme and cotton grass -
The bleating sheep, the lapwings in the valley of the Swale -
Such glowing coloured scenery of moorland and of dale!

Hovering like a kestrel over once famous Reeth,
The remains of its lead mines all strewn beneath,
Smelt mills and chimneys in lonely ravines,
Their workings still visible in decaying machines:

"Remember the miners who toiled all their lives
To bring up their children, look after their wives.
May we always honour the folk of this place -
Ignoring their stories would be a disgrace."

Leaving the harshness of Harkenside Moor,
Flying north across Teesdale, then on to Tow Law
Where Inkerman Colliery was worked to the bone
As the scarred blackened faces of miners have shown -

North-east to Cornsay, Hamsteels, Quebec -
Collieries with names we should never forget -
Horden and Rainton, Blackhall and Pittington,
Then flying east towards Shotton and Easington,

Where opened the colliery in 1899,
Closed after a century - a painful decline,
And not until tragedy caused major strife,
Eighty-three trees marking each loss of life.

"In Durham's fair county I've seen many signs
Of cottages, pitheads, settlements, mines -
The land's been reclaimed, trees and cereals grown,
But many lives lost of people unknown!

"In steel I'll commemorate all mining folk
Who toiled to serve us in black airless smoke.
As a statue I'll speak to those from afar,
'Remember the miners as you pass in your car.'"

The angel declaims a strong message for all,
Standing so proudly, standing so tall,
Pointing the way from industrial strife
To a cleaner and greener and kinder new life.

Lots of oohs and aahs from everyone, and a gentle ripple of applause. "Well done, Tammy! Great stuff."

The afternoon gave us a wonderful cycle ride over the Lincolnshire Wolds, the so-called breadbasket of England. Vast golden fields, stretching out for miles in every direction, towards Grimsby and fishing to the east, Scunthorpe and steel mills to the west, but we were splicing between them with the sun shining down upon us in all its August glory.

We arrived in Barnetby le Wold at the largest bed-and-breakfast I'd ever been to. Not only did the main house have seventeen rooms but there was also an annexe across the road which accommodated the whole of our group. It had its own dining room and kitchen so we could be completely independent for meals. The landlady invited us to help ourselves to the raspberries which were growing in profusion in the back garden. There was a Chinese takeaway in the village which served us well for dinner, and we bought milk and cornflakes from the One-Stop across the road for breakfast.

Rosie chose to read out her poem that evening, so I slipped in quickly with:

Then Rosie spoke - I find it hard to write
About this flower, this angel of delight.
(My words, you'll note, are totally unworthy
To capture Rosie, creature so unearthly.)
Sweet loving wife to Phil, you lucky man!
And friend to all - (poor lines - at least they scan).

"I'm not sure about 'angel of delight' - makes me sound like a pudding! Anyway, here goes."

The Song of Belinda who campaigned for Nature

Belinda as a little girl was blessed with long blonde hair,
Her eyes were blue and sparkling, her face was round and fair.
She loved to play in nature, climb high into the trees
And there she'd talk to angels as they fluttered in the leaves.

She kept this as a secret from her family and friends:
"On the wisdom of the angels all my life depends.
They guide me and support me - a source of endless light
And whenever life disturbs me, they always put me right."

Her parents, Mike and Gwenda, were delighted with their child,
And even as an infant Mother Nature on her smiled:
"I feel a special closeness, as if she were my own,
One who'll love me dearly, every root and every stone."

From childhood Belinda could not cope with eating meat.
The very thought repelled her. "People really ought to treat
Animals and birds and fish with more respect and care.
One day I'll speak on their behalf - lead protests - so beware!"

When she was still a little girl she formed her own campaign
To speak up for the innocent, the victims of man's shame.
"Respect the rights of animals! Nature is our friend,
We need to love and nurture her, for on her we do depend."

She became a well-known figure in the counties and the shires.
Her message was so simple. "All that one requires
Is a vegetarian diet, in respect of Nature's laws."
She spoke in towns and cities, in the hills and on the shores.

Her message was appealing to a growing band of folk,
It challenged and inspired them every time she spoke.
"It's time to change our habits, perhaps our way of life
To one which is less harmful, reducing stress and strife."

She led parades at Marble Arch, rallies in Oxford Square.
"Get out into the countryside, take deep lungfuls of fresh air,
Speak to the cows, the sheep, the deer in words both sweet and calm,
Say how much you love them, and never wish them harm."

She often went out on a limb, led wintry midnight walks
Through starlit fields and forests, engaged in Nature talks.
"We love your wild places, and all your windy weather,
Frost and ice, gales and storms, all wrapped up together!"

In summer months she'd amble through meadows decked with flowers,
Talking to the mice and voles in sunshine and in showers.
"You lovely things, so innocent, the worm, the wren, the shrew,
The earwig, slug and errant ant - yes, we love you too!"

Her followers increased tenfold, a cheerful merry band,
From Portsmouth to the Isle of Skye and Ireland's emerald land.
They walked through ripening fields under the Harvest Moon
And everywhere they travelled they sang their special tune:

"O Spirit of Mother Nature, provider of such wealth,
We're grateful for your bounty, the source of all our health."

They sang this song which lingered long for those who heard its strain,
And they in turn took up the tune like a national refrain...

Imagine if you can that this story I have told
Could happen in some fashion, and thereby, might unfold
A kinder brighter future, which nobody would hinder,
To realise a better way - all thanks to you, Belinda!

We all laughed - what a lovely "green" poem! And the ending linked nicely with Tammy's, too. Good night!

Sunday

We had eaten our cornflakes and were on the road by 8:00 o'clock - a record. There was a long pull-up out of Barnetby which was grim but then we sailed on breezily, along a high ridge road with the fields ripe for harvesting on either side. Once we had to make way for a convoy of massive agricultural machines (big yellow German ones called Ploeger, with 'Achtung' written on the back, and slightly smaller red ones called Sumo) under police escort.

We bypassed the villages of Grasby and Searby, ending up in Caistor, a picturesque Georgian town, slightly run-down but gradually being restored to its former state of glory. Summer Sundays in Lincolnshire are dozy days, and nothing was open, so coffee would have to wait.

Henry recommended that we visit the All Saints Church in Walesby, otherwise known as the Ramblers Church.

"Honestly, it will be worth the detour," and so it proved. Down into a valley, where the waysides were colourful with wild scabious of a delicate blue, yellow vetch, red hawthorn and black elderberries - and flurries of sparrows leading the way from hedge to hedge - until we arrived at a fingerpost pointing the way to the church. We leant our bikes against the fence, and plodded up an unpromising dark muddy track where the sunlight hardly entered. But then the sound of church bells chiming the tenth hour of the day drew us on.

We emerged from the path into a typical English country churchyard full of stone monuments, well cared for grounds and a small medieval church built of honey-coloured sandstone, set on a slight hill and bathed in morning sunlight. There was hardly a breath of wind to disturb the peace and tranquillity. We walked around in silence.

I came across a signboard saying, *In 2014, the PCC and Friends of the Old Church decided to adopt the 'Caring for God's Acre' approach to churchyard management. This allows the beauty of flower rich grassland and the animal life it supports to be seen and enjoyed. It allows wildflowers to set seed and increase, and it provides food for butterflies and other insects.* How wonderful, I thought.

I suggested it was time for a poem, as we lay down or sat in the grass, listening to the crickets chirrup and savouring the sweet smells of yesterday's mowings.

"I have a song to sing, oh!" announced Don gaily, quoting Gilbert and Sullivan, "but of course I won't sing it. Come, gather round all, and make yourselves comfortable. It's all about one of my childhood heroes, King Alfred the Great."

"Wait a moment," I called out, and rummaging in my bag I found the introductory lines to my dear husband.

There was a teacher, short and bald and fat -
But, truth to tell, he's so much more than that.
As husbands go, he's answered all my wishes:
He's paid the bills, changed nappies, washed the dishes.
But most of all he's fun and makes me laugh,
And parties on: "Let's have another half!"

"Hmm. I only half enjoyed that. Swiftly moving on then."

The Ballad of Alfred the Great

Our island has been ruled by many a queen and king
But only Alfred is 'The Great', so it is of him I sing.
He suffered many hardships, but whenever all seemed lost
He put his faith in the Lord above, and did not count the cost.

A cultured and a pious man, preferring the quiet life,
The story I will tell you is one of struggle and strife.
Before his reign the Vikings came, their terror had begun,
They drove him from his palace - and he was on the run.

His kingdom, known as Wessex, stretched from Cornwall to distant Kent
But now the marshes of Somerset were his shrunken realm's extent.
From being lord of all from the Tamar to the Thames,
His rule had shrivelled to nothing, just family and close friends.

Alfred, son of Aethelwulf, with all his followers ran,
While behind him the robber Vikings spread out in a fan,
Searching for the fleeing king, letting out the cry:
"Your time is up. The choice is stark. Yield to us, or die!"

The Viking lord, named Guthrum, was merciless and cruel,
He'd captured Wessex violently, maintained an iron rule,
His reign was one of terror, commanding loyalty through fear,
While Alfred ruled with love and grace, holding his people dear.

Guthrum by his victory maintained the upper hand
While Alfred with his soldiers skulked in Somerset's sodden land.
Breathing mist before a fire, wrapped in a threadbare cloak,
Alfred sent out messages: 'I'll save you yet, good folk!

"Come, my loyal people, join me in the fray,
Together we will rout this man. He'll live to rue the day.
This murderous band of villains will get their just deserts -
With all our skill and courage we will hit them where it hurts!"

Alfred arrived at Athelney in March 878
A dismal island fortress for a man of royal estate.
360 paces long by some 50 paces wide,
This barren misty fenland was where the king would hide

With barely a hundred followers, all loyal to the core,
But scarcely a match for the Vikings - "I need five thousand more!"
Here on these wooded islands, traversed by tortuous streams,
Alfred's name became legend, entered the world of dreams.

While sheltering in a swineherd's hut - for rest and comfort yearning -
Alfred failed to tend the cakes, never knew that they were burning.
"Wake up, varlet," the man's wife said, "What's this appalling smell?
"Look what you've done: these cakes are ruined - only fit for Hell!"

"Pardon me, good lady, I dozed and failed to see
The smoke and ruination while I lay back dreamily.
This failure is a lesson about fulfilling my proper role.
To arise and vanquish the Vikings is now my cherished goal!"

Both kings arrayed their armies high above the Wiltshire Plain,
It would be a savage test, but with everything to gain.
Alfred's men were yeomen, prepared to risk their lives,
Loyal untrained soldiers bearing cudgels, staves and knives.

The Northmen waited with painted shields, standing in solid line,
Spears prickling out through the wall like a ferocious porcupine.
The army of Wessex approached. "Don't let the wall spread out!
"Drum on the rim of your shields, hold your nerve. Now, SHOUT!"

Boasts and menacing threats rang out as the lines converged,
The impact of wood, bone and muscle as heaving soldiers merged.
The fighting was bloody and brutal, the Vikings could not hold fast:
The Saxons piled into their midst and emerged triumphant at last.

By winning the Battle of Edington Alfred had humbled their king,
But instead of reprisal and vengeance, showed forgiveness - a rare thing!
"All I demand of your people is that baptism you will receive.
Abandon your gods, become Christians like us - in mercy and justice believe!"

Guthrum accepted the bargain, for this was abundantly clear:
The God of the Christians had triumphed where his had failed to appear.
Alfred had vanquished Guthrum with the edge of the sharpened sword
But now he sought to convert him through the power of God's word.

As the thirty white-clad Northmen towards the church processed
They all abandoned their gods, their many errors confessed,
The priest signed each with the cross, placed salt upon his tongue,
And with immersion in the font their new life had begun.

When all the baptismal ceremonies were properly completed,
The Viking king along with his men were generously treated.
Gold and silver treasures were showered on them all,
Celebration and lavish feasts took place in the royal hall.

"This message I convey to you," said Alfred to the Danes,
"If you cooperate with us, then everybody gains.
Reneging on our deal will only bring hostility,
So let us now swear amity and an end to all duplicity."

Guthrum, now called Aethelstan, with his warriors marched away.
Alfred, sighing with relief, said, "Let this peace hold sway.
I feel all times of conflict are like wasting precious fuel -
From now on let me concentrate on cultural renewal."

Although the rest of his long life was never free from war,
Alfred's primary focus was on learning and good law.
His name may be remembered as the one who burnt the cakes,
But the moral's very simple, to learn from our mistakes.

I think one or two people had dozed off, possibly more, because the applause was rather muted. I didn't want Don to feel discouraged so I gave him a hug and a kiss and said,

"That was lovely, darling. I'm proud of you!"

On we went to Market Rasen, where we all dived in to a café for coffee and a pastry. And the experience was so blissful that we repeated it. Hey ho, never mind the calories! Anyway, what have I got to lose?

At this point we reacquainted ourselves with the National Cycle routes for we soon picked up NCN1 which would take us all the way to Lincoln. It was flat and easy-going, and we found ourselves passing through some oddly-named villages like Linwood and Lissington, Wickenby and Snelland, Reasby and Scother. It was a mixed kind of day, sometimes hot, sometimes cool, mostly dry, a bit windy – and one extremely heavy shower. At one point Phil, who was leading, braked suddenly and we all drew up quickly behind him.

"Help yourselves, boys and girls," he announced. A heavily-laden apple tree was leaning over the fence of an orchard, and there was plenty of fruit on the grass verge for us to have a healthy snack. After that we decided we would press on to Lincoln, find our accommodation and have a late lunch.

Gentle ups and downs, a few twists and turns in the villages, plodding on and on - and then, all of a sudden, Phil braked again beside a fence. Pointing west over a golden field of corn, he cried out, "Look, everyone!"

And there on the distant horizon was the unmistakable silhouette of Lincoln Cathedral, looking tiny but standing out proudly, a beacon for miles around in every direction. We lingered there for several minutes, shading our eyes against the sunlight and marveling at the work of man, in particular William the Conqueror, who commanded the construction of this cathedral nearly a thousand years ago.

Soon it was time to move on, and we arrived in the city at 2:00 o'clock. Rosie had cleverly organised accommodation for us at the University. Our hall of residence was called Cygnet Wharf, and we would each have a student room to ourselves. Cycling through the city and trying not to be lured by its obvious attractions, we headed straight there and found our rooms in the building which overlooked Brayford Pool. The University was built on reclaimed land in the mid-90s so it still had a modern fresh look. My room was next to Don's on the third floor, and I loved unpacking my bits and pieces as if I were a student again in Freshers' Week. It was much better than our accommodation in Durham nearly fifty years ago. To start with, the bed was twice the size, as was the storage space, it had its own shower and loo, and a spacious desk with plenty of sockets and lots of shelves above. Something hankered in me to start being a student again, but the idea soon disappeared when Don knocked on my door and said, "Ready for lunch, and an explore?"

Three free hours on a warm Sunday exploring an ancient city with all its street entertainers, riverside walks, medieval gateways, old streets and an independent coffee shop shaded by six magnificent London plane trees in full leaf - bliss! For a while we watched an extraordinary Irish jig dancer doing high kicks and tap dancing on a small square piece of wood. We admired a shiny metal sculpture of two dancers spanning the river, and a couple of folk singers in St Barnabas Square touched us with their plaintive duet. The streets were full of milling tourists enjoying a lazy afternoon. We ate Cornish pasties and ice creams, took selfies, posted them on Facebook and waited for the 'likes' and smiley faces. We promised ourselves the more 'proper' tourist activities, such as the cathedral and the castle, tomorrow - but for today, we drifted in the sunshine like everybody else.

That evening we gathered in the Minerva Building with other visiting guests on their own holiday courses, and joined the buffet queue for lasagne and chips (topped up with a selection from the salad bar), followed by a large slice of strawberry cake and rather poor coffee.

I had a quiet word with Henry and asked him if he would like to read his poem this evening. He reached inside his pocket and pulled out a few scrappy sheets of paper. He looked extremely nervous and twitchy.

"It's still not finished, but this is the right time, now that we're in Lincoln," he said gloomily. "I've been dreading this moment all day but I can't put it off any longer. Okay, Margot, set the ball rolling."

We found a quietish corner away from the other diners, drew some chairs into a rough circle and soon everyone was quiet for my little preamble:

There was a sculptor of worldwide renown
Whose marble forms one sees in many a town.
A modern Michelangelo, I would say,
Whose flawless works are on permanent display.
A cut above us ordinary chaps
But loneliness the price he pays, perhaps.

"Well, it's interesting that you should say that, Margot. I don't mean putting me on a level with Michelangelo, but I think quite possibly we were both loners, and that's a heavy price to pay."

Henry cleared his throat, looked around at everyone, adjusted his glasses, then took them off again, hesitating.

"Sorry, but I must point out that Margot gave me some help with the rhymes and rhythms of the opening verses. The rest of it's my own, which I have been working on overnight while you've all been asleep, but it's still unfinished."

He paused again.

"Okay, here goes."

Confessions of a Lad from Lincolnshire

There was a lad from Lincolnshire, Henry was his name,
He was a fortune-hunter, sought prosperity and fame,
He made some stupid blunders which you'll certainly deplore,
Lost his peace of mind and happiness which nothing can restore.

He had a certain talent with paintbrush, pen and ink,
Could capture someone's likeness as quick as you can blink,
He tried his hand at sculpture in wood and bronze and stone,
Displayed a natural aptitude as soon as he was shown.

Success and wealth came quickly to this young man from the Wolds,
He won prestigious prizes, nearly all his works were sold.
In a saturated market, facing serious competition,
Young Henry's fame grew rapidly with every exhibition.

In Lincoln town he settled down with gallery and wife,
A lovely girl called Angela, devoted her whole life
To make her husband happy, she bore a lovely son,
She gave him every comfort - little Harry was such fun!

But Henry felt restricted by Lincoln's narrow ways,
"I need a bigger city where I can dazzle and amaze.
Let's move north to Edinburgh, take the Festival apart,
Make an even bigger fortune with my sculpture, with my art."

Angela was horrified to hear her husband say
That he'd had enough of Lincoln, wanted to move away.
"We're settled here, we have our friends, we're well served by the schools.
Give up our happy way of life? We really would be fools!"

Henry was quite adamant: "Lincolnshire's so flat!
I'm uninspired, I'm bored and tired of Wolds, and that is that.
I need a broader canvas where I can spread my wings,
Some mountains, lakes and rivers, waterfalls and springs.

"Scotland is appealing with its rugged open spaces,
I'm sure you would adore a change - completely different places.
Its wild unbroken countryside, purple heather on the hills,
And its stormy skies at sunset - these would cure me of all ills."

But Angela wouldn't hear of it: "We're happy and we're blessed
With a lovely home and child. Let's be grateful, be at rest
Without hankering for any more. I have nothing more to say.
If you want to go to Scotland, by yourself you'll have to stay."

Did he love his wife and baby? Did he think of them at all?
He must have been possessed by some obsessive inner call
That blinded him to duty, love and simple common sense:
He made the break, deserted them and travelled far from thence.

"And that's all I've managed to write – sorry."

There was a long pause, a mixture of disbelief and embarrassment. Eventually Judith broke the silence.

"So you went to Edinburgh and lived there, by yourself?"

"Yes. I had a few artist friends there so I knew what I was doing. And I had some relatives there. As you know, my parents were Scottish."

Once Judith had broken the ice, we all started chipping in with questions.

"How long ago was this, Henry?"

"Oh, at least thirty years ago. I'm 65 now so Angela will be 62."

"And Harry will be about 30?"

"Yes, that's right."

"And you've seen neither of them since?"

"That's right," he said quietly. "It's been quite painful dredging it all up again, as well as trying to write it down," - he slapped the back of his hand across the crumpled pieces of paper - "but I have tried to give you a true account."

I looked across at Winnie, her face white with fury as though she had been deceived by Henry for the last few years. She had after all taken him in and given him a home, yet all the time there was this secret he'd never divulged. But she remained silent. Controlling my own feelings of utter disbelief, I put on my "sweet" voice and said, "I really don't understand how you could have done that, Henry. You mean, you abandoned your wife and child, never to see them again, so you could pursue an artist's life in the wilds of Scotland. I'm amazed… in fact I can hardly believe anyone could do such a thing. Didn't you have any feelings for them? I presume you supported them."

Henry had sat down by this time, holding his head in his hands which were resting on his knees. Without looking up, he said, "Oh yes, I sent money on a regular basis. Look, I don't feel in the least bit proud about what I've done, Margot, and in the end I have paid quite a heavy price."

"How do you mean?"

He looked up, holding his hands outspread as he tried to explain himself. "I strongly believed that I had a special talent, a genius, in fact. I know it sounds incredibly arrogant of me to say this, but that was how I felt, and I wanted to develop it in a more inspiring place than Lincolnshire which I was finding increasingly claustrophobic and stifling. It was just so flat everywhere. I came to hate the little narrow streets and lanes of the city – in fact the very parts which everybody loves so much. Also I was inspired by a book I had read, called *The Moon and Sixpence* by Somerset Maugham which is based on the life of the artist, Paul Gauguin. He left his wife and family to devote his life to painting. He left Europe for Tahiti because he thought that was the only way he could develop his talent. The title of the book comes from a phrase in a letter by Somerset Maugham which I've always remembered: "If you look on the ground in search of sixpence, you don't look up, and so miss the moon." I knew I would never be satisfied with quiet domesticity in Lincoln for the rest of my life – but Angela couldn't see that. Now I am not blaming her at all, but… well, there it was…"

There was another long pause, until Winnie spoke up in a decidedly icy tone. "At least your career turned out well. Nice for you."

"Yes, I suppose so. Fame and success and money. But I have blanked out everything else, and I have to live with this gnawing guilt every day of my life. I sometimes wonder how I sleep at nights."

He took out his handkerchief, blew his nose and looked round at all of us saying, "Sorry, everyone. Talk about a party pooper! I'm really sorry."

Rosie, who was sitting next to him, took his hand.

"We're your friends, Henry," she said quietly, "and we want to help you. Is there anything we can do that will help?"

"There is something you can do," Henry said after a short pause. "Angela is here in this city, I know she is, because she loved Lincoln and would never leave it. I'm quite sure she's still here, so I want to find her and say I'm sorry. We do have another day here, so I would be tremendously grateful if ..."

He stopped to wipe his eyes, and I could feel the waves of sympathy going out towards him. Don spoke up.

"Where could we start, Henry? Thirty years is a long time."

Henry shook himself a bit as he does when he becomes excited.

"I could take you where we had our gallery and we could start from there. She was interested in the Cathedral and she was interested in the local antiquarian bookshops. Her whole life revolved around Lincoln, and I feel if you - or some of you, at any rate - might be prepared to accompany me, because I couldn't do it on my own, we might find a few clues, a trail, perhaps, which might eventually..."

He tailed off, probably realising that it was a hopeless task. Cynthia chimed in, wanting to encourage him and always having a great sense of purpose. "Come on, everyone, let's give it a go. We have all tomorrow here, and I think it would be time very well spent, looking for Angela."

A few people agreed, but Winnie was not one of them. "You can count me out," she said. "I'm sorry, but I don't want any part of it. I'm not going to waste my time on a wild goose chase. Peter and I have better things to do, don't we, love?"

The evening broke up on a somewhat disharmonious note, with whisperings and mutterings in a few corners, which was so unlike us. But Rosie remained next to Henry, comforting him.

"Shall we go to our room, Margot?" asked Don, leaning over in my direction.

"Yes, let's."

Monday

The following morning, when Don and I arrived for breakfast, I saw Winnie, Peter, James and David at a table together. We went over and had a chat with them, because it looked as though they were planning something.

"We're hiring a car to visit a few places while we're here," said Peter.

"Good idea," said Don.

"Are you really going to try and help Henry find Angela?" asked James.

"We'll see what turns up this morning," I said. "I'm still in a slight state of disbelief about yesterday evening, so we're not making any plans at the moment. Anyway, have a lovely day, and we'll meet up this evening."

By 10:00 o'clock, nine of us were standing in Lincoln High Street ready to take instructions from Henry. We were approaching the task in a serious way, but I suspect we all saw the funny side of it as well.

"Thank you very much, everyone. Is it all right if I lead the way?" and off we went in the direction of the cathedral.

Our search began in earnest at the foot of a narrow uphill street called THE STRAIT (a curved wrought-iron arch, topped by the famous Lincoln imp, linked the buildings either side), and very soon we came to a small art gallery on the left-hand side.

"This was my shop, and that was where we lived," said Henry excitedly, pointing up to the first floor. But on making enquiries, nobody had heard of the artist Henry Fletcher, or of his wife or son. Henry was not too put out by this.

"Of course, Angela didn't work here - in fact, she wasn't particularly interested in art. Her real interest was books, and there was a shop up here..." he said, looking up the cobbled street, now bathed in sunlight. "Come on, follow me," which we dutifully did.

Soon there was an A board propped up on the cobblestones with the words "Antique Books, 2-3 Steep Hill" in swirling writing. The wooden lintel to the doorway bore the words JEWS COURT.

"This is it! They'll know her in here."

But they didn't, although as we browsed our way through the various rooms and Rosie chatted to the proprietor, there was a sudden cry from Phil: "Look at this! *Hidden Lincoln* by Angela Fletcher."

"Let me see," called Henry, running over and looking over Phil's shoulder. "Yes, that's hers. I'd forgotten all about it. You see, I'm not making this up."

"We never doubted you for a moment, old chap," said Phil, patting him on the shoulder. "We've simply got to find the lady behind the name. Come on, there are probably a few more bookshops up here, aren't there?"

"Lots more!" said Henry, and stormed out.

"Not now there aren't," said the proprietor, but Henry didn't hear that, and when we followed him up the street, we saw his crestfallen face staring into a bijou-looking place on the right-hand side.
"Oh, no! It's gone - look!"

I couldn't help a burst of laughter when I saw what it now was: *Beauty Parlour: Liposuction and Exfoliation.*

"Oh dear, this is looking hopeless," he said dejectedly. "I'm sorry, this is turning into a wild goose chase. We'd better give up and go home."

Now Angus stepped in.

"Come on, Henry, don't lose heart. Didn't you say she used to go to Evensong? Let's go up to the cathedral. Maybe somebody there will know her."

We had a little conference and decided to split up and make enquiries at every place nearby, which included the cathedral, the castle, the Tourist Information Office, shops and cafés, particularly asking people who looked old or local if anyone knew about a certain Angela Fletcher. We could do some sightseeing at the same time, then meet at 1:00 o'clock for refreshments in the nearby BookStop Café on Christ's Hospital Terrace to compare notes.

The time passed pleasantly enough but, sad to say, we drew a total blank.

Our chosen venue was housed in an old barrel-vaulted room with white-washed ceiling (medieval, 1170-1190, the young man informed us), situated under the Imperial Tea and Coffee Company which not only supplied the raw materials for drinks but also the cakes, by way of a connecting rugged stone stairway marked STAFF ONLY. The cakes were displayed in an elegant round triple-tiered glass cabinet, lit by twinkling fairy lights. Soft piped music added to the soothing atmosphere. I sank into a deep black sofa, ordered an Americano and a flapjack, and settled down for a long stay and a good read.

But Henry soon flopped down next to me on the sofa, wiped his brow and appeared inconsolable. How could I cheer him up? I had an idea. "Come on, Henry, let's have a look at the cakes."

Now if he has a weakness it is for a slice of Victoria Sponge, so I dragged him up and we went over to the glass cabinet. It had the desired effect for I began to see a slight gleam in his eyes.

"Oh, my word!" he exclaimed. "Just look at those, Margot! How does anyone make such wonderful-looking cakes. I wouldn't know where to start."

He make a long hard study of each tier in turn.

"Excuse me," he said, turning to the young man, "I suppose you wouldn't by any chance have a Victoria Sponge. I just fancy a slice with a cup of tea."

"I'll ring upstairs. Wait a moment," and he made a quick call. "Yes, she'll be down in a moment."

"Oh, good!" and a broad smile spread over his face. "Does she bake all the cakes?"

"Yes, Angela is our wonderful baker."

"Angela?"

And in a moment, the STAFF ONLY sign was unhooked and a short, slightly plump lady, wearing a lacy pinafore, with long wavy silver hair appeared at the foot of the stone staircase, bearing a large Victoria Sponge cake.

"Angela!"

"My goodness, it can't be! Henry!"

Poor Henry! He was desperately trying to make overtures to Angela, but was all the while acutely aware of our presence. He hopped from foot to foot, dithering and not knowing what to say. Fortunately

Angela took him calmly by the hand. "We need to speak privately, Henry," and started leading him back up the stone steps. He gave us a little wave and, with a weak "Bye, everyone, bye," he disappeared - and that was that.

It was, I suppose, a satisfactory outcome to the morning's adventure, even if it left a large number of unanswered questions. However, since we were all still enjoying the comfort of this cosy literary café, I thought it was time for a literary tale, and I knew Angus was prepared.

"Listen, everyone," I said, quickly changing the subject, "Here is my prelude to the poem from Angus, who I know is at the ready."

Now, Angus, tell a tale of merriment,
We know you are a literary gent.
Some history, philosophy or song,
A story that's instructive - not too long.
But as you know your Shakespeare through and through
No doubt his name appears - over to you!

"You've read me like a book, Margot! I have written this for my godson, in an attempt to interest him in the Swan of Stratford. But, with your permission, I would like to try it out on you good people first. So here goes."

The Song of William Shakespeare

It was upon St George's Day in 1564
That I was born - Will Shakespeare - remembered evermore
As the gentleman from Stratford who wrote plays in London town
For the rough-and-tumble commoners, as well as for the Crown.

Stratford was a thriving place beside the river Avon
Where John my father was alderman, of honourable reputation.
He'd married Mary Arden from a farming family,
Hence middle-class my background, of respectable gentry.

I was the eldest son, of siblings I had seven,
My Grammar School upbringing was very far from heaven.
The day began at six o'clock and lasted for twelve hours,
And with only two short intervals it taxed my childish powers.

I found it hard to stay awake, absorbing so much learning -
My boyish spirits stifled, for freedom I was yearning.
The discipline was very tough, beatings were the rule,
No wonder "every boy crept like snail unwillingly to school".

Queen Elizabeth was thirty in the year that I was born,
Five years she'd reigned, thirty-nine to come, the longest of them all.
Protestant daughter of Henry, she suffered excommunication,
"A bastard!" claimed the Catholics - some plotted assassination.

Intelligent and cultured, her life was no bed of clover
For her cousin Mary, Queen of Scots, was seeking to take over.
She never took a husband, so the matter of succession
Was a constitutional nightmare, a major preoccupation.

But I was thus far ignorant, and in my early life,
When father was a glover, and mother a loving wife,
My greatest childhood pleasure was to see the travelling plays
With actors on the backs of carts, dressed in colourful array.

These I found entrancing, they fired my imagination -
For my future as a playwright - what a source of inspiration!
My father was Town Bailiff and I was only five
When the players first came to Stratford and brought the town alive.

At age fifteen, school over, with a boisterous constitution,
I poached for deer at Charlecote Park - they threatened prosecution!
With roving eye, I fell in love with one Anne Hathaway,
Desiring her with all my heart - we married one autumn day

When I was eighteen years of age, twenty-six was she.
Susanna, our first, was born in 1583.
Judith and Hamnet, bonny twins, later on arrived -
Then silence...about nine years, no record of me survived.

I turn up next in London in 1592,
Determined to make my fortune as a playwright but - oh, phew!
The city stank of sewage, the streets were a disgrace,
Plague was never far away - "Get me out of this place!"

Ignoring the smells, the discomfort, with a destiny to fulfil
I entered the world of literature, conscious I had some skill
At penning ingenious verses to appeal to the city's bright sparks,
I was young and impetuous - and also up for some larks.

My first steps into playwriting were comedy and history:
"Love's Labours Lost" and "Titus" - how the words flew was a mystery.
"Henry VI parts 1, 2, 3" plus "Venus and Adonis",
A poem that captured the hearts of many lovesick worthies!

By the time that I was 28, I'd earned a reputation
As "mellifluous" and "honey-tongued" - but also indignation
From certain jealous rivals, ever eager to show
That I was a country bumpkin, merely an "upstart crow".

My career was in the ascendant, I joined the Chamberlain's Men,
And added "Richard III" with my unerring pen.
"A Comedy of Errors", "The Taming of the Shrew" -
Such were my early works, and I earned a pound or two.

In fifteen hundred and ninety-nine I donned a different robe
As joint proprietor of the stage famously called The Globe.
We were a well-established team, showed wit and renowned facility
For the widest range of dramas and dazzling versatility.

Our watchwords were variety, excitement and emotion,
Laughter, tears and conflict, performed with true devotion.
And when we played at Court for Elizabeth our queen,
Ah, joy was then unbounded, the fulfilment of our dream!

I loved creating characters from merry Sir John Falstaff,
To Romeo and Juliet, making audiences cry and laugh.
Using the broadest brushstrokes I painted a varied cast
With every shade of colour upon a canvas vast.

My history plays reflected the problems of our time
Mixing comedy with tragedy to expose some villain's crime,
Soon I turned to darker themes in plays both raw and fraught,
Wrote soliloquies where characters revealed many a complex thought.

I explored man's baser nature and developed a bleaker strain,
"Macbeth", and "Othello" - dark tragedies - alongside "Hamlet the Dane".
My final phase was softer - romances with hints of magic,
"A Winter's Tale" and "The Tempest", but still with elements tragic.

From London home to Stratford often I had returned,
To share with my beloved family the money I had earned.
Now I recall our saddest time when our young Hamnet died,
He was only a lad of eleven - such cruelty! - how we cried.

At length, my creativity spent, I needed a quieter life
To enjoy the comforts of home with my daughters and loving wife,
It takes its toll, dear reader, producing plays for the stage,
A young man's game - exhausting! - I was starting to feel my age.

We settled in New Place in 1610
Where I happily followed a new regimen:
Developed an estate with cattle and hay,
Now a farmer instead - a new role to play!

I kept up my friendships with literary folk,
Asked them to stay, shared some story or joke,
A life then of ease and leisured pursuits,
In Warwickshire county, the place of my roots.

I departed my life in 1616
The day of St George, as my birth day had been.
Anxious to lie undisturbed in my grave,
These lines on my tombstone I requested engraved:

Good frend for Jesus sake forbeare
To digg the dust enclosed heare;
Bleste be ye man yt spare these stones
And curst be he yt moves my bones

Posterity has been kind to me: the plays have lasted well,
Wherever they are still performed they cast a magic spell.
So thank you humbly, gentlefolk, for listening to my song,
And may your lives be heaven-blest, free from all pain and wrong.

A loud round of applause from us and the other coffee-drinkers who were equally entranced. And Angus of course loves an audience. It was a supreme performance.

xxx

"And that was the last we saw of him," I told Winnie when we were having a pre-dinner drink in the Minerva Building. "They exchanged a few words, then she ushered him away upstairs, and he didn't reappear."

"Lucky man! I hope she has it in her heart to forgive him. Do you think we'll see him again this holiday?"

"There's really no knowing. But he'll have to return to his rooms at some point and collect his things. I'm sure he will be in touch soon. Anyway, how are you feeling now? Did you enjoy your day?"

"Yes, we had a lovely relaxing time, exploring a bit, walking, talking. I really have a soft spot for David, particularly now he's lost his parents, and I think he found it helpful talking about it. Henry came up in conversation, of course, and I started thinking about the mistakes I had made in my life which still preyed on my mind. It dawned on me how courageous it was of Henry to unburden himself like that. It was still a terrible thing to do but...well, perhaps there was more to it, which we shall never know."

Tammy appeared at that moment.

"Come on, you two, and join the queue or there won't be any food left. And then we have story time!"
After supper Phil announced that he'd had a text from Henry.

"He says thank you very much, everyone. He's cleared out his room - although he doesn't say where he is staying! - but he'll definitely be joining us for our final meal in York."

Now it was Cynthia's turn, and she looked very shy as I read out:

A lady then rose, fair Cynthia by name,
"And fair by nature, too!" you all exclaim.
Music, singing, dance - and yoga too -
Yet flowers remain her greatest joy, it's true.
Some floral tale of friendship now she'll tell,
So spin your yarn and weave a magic spell.

"I'd already told Margot about my poem, so her introduction gives a slight hint of what's to come."

She stood up and recited:

The Song of Two Roses

Is friendship the rose in the garden,
Warmed by the sun up above,
Watered by tender devotion,
Sweetened by petals of love?

Is it the weaving of heart-strings,
Withstanding the buffets of time,
Streams of love flowing together
Captured in words and in rhyme?

One remembers great friendships in history,
Fictional, fanciful, true,
Some legendary, some mythological,
All examples to me and to you.

The Owl and the Pussycat's famous,
And so's that of Morecombe and Wise,
Haydn and Mozart, Achilles and Patroclus -
All bonded by long-lasting ties.

I sing of a flowering friendship
With a floribund-hybrid theme,
It concerns two affectionate roses
Who appeared in a wonderful dream.

Their names were Belinda and Joseph,
Shy friends in a well-manured bed.
Joseph, a pink floribunda,
Took courage one morning and said:

"Belinda, my heart is near bursting
For the fondness I feel for you.
Your petals so velvety crimson,
Your leaves such a glossy green hue!"

Belinda, a prize-winning hybrid,
Blushed to hear these remarks from her friend.
"To me your floriferous blooming
Is a pink bushy joy without end.

"You're so hardy and sturdy beside me,
I feel your support day and night."
Said Joseph, "Your deep fragrant perfume
Gives me endless odiferous delight."

Their friendship became ever deeper,
Smoothed by the morning dew,
Held in the soil of measureless love,
Affectionate, tender and true.

And as they continued to flourish
Growing closer and closer each day;
They cast a spell over neighbouring plants,
Charming their problems away.

The garden became ever-stronger,
Resistant, robust, disease-free,
Vibrant in colour with sturdier stems,
Every flower, every shrub and tree.

Belinda and Joseph were happy
To see the effect they imparted,
Grateful as well for the fortunate day
When side by side they were planted.

I woke from my dream at that moment,
And felt a soft breeze in my hair
For the window was open, the sun streaming in
And the scent of a rose on the air.

If there had been any disharmony among us that day, Cynthia's poem dispelled it instantly. There really was nothing more to say except "Good night, sweet dreams - see you in the morning."

Tuesday

As you know, I don't do illness, by which I mean I don't talk about it. So it's enough to say that I had a bad night, and in the morning I told Don: "I'm sorry, dear heart, but I won't be able to cycle today."

Quite unperturbed, he said, "I'm sorry, love. I'll book train tickets back to York."

"No, I didn't mean that. You never know, I might be all right tomorrow. I really want to see this through, but is there a way I can go to the next place by train?"

"I'll ring Phil."

I lay there as still as possible, listening to the early-morning cries of seagulls, imagining them wheeling over Brayford Pool.

In a few moments he came back. "He says that he can take you by train to Scunthorpe via Bartleby where we spent that one night. From there, it's only six miles to his mum's village of Winterton. You might feel well enough to cycle a small distance by late afternoon, but if not he can easily organise a friend to take you to her house."

"That sounds fine."

"The only thing is, his mum won't want any visitors until late afternoon, which means spending the morning here, and catching a train at about 2:00 o'clock."

"That's perfect. I need to sleep. You go down to breakfast and tell the others. I don't want anything."

Fortunately the feeling of sickness was passing and I think I must have dozed a little. The next thing I knew, the door was opening and Don appeared, followed by Phil. They sat beside me on the bed and Don held my hand. Before he spoke, I said: "I want you to cycle with the others, so that I can hear about the day firsthand from you."

"That was what I was going to ask you. Phil's quite happy to look after you today, and we'll all turn up at Winterton later and spend the evening together."

So that was the arrangement. I didn't want to see anyone else, so Phil went off to find out about trains while Don packed up the room. I very gradually got up and dressed, feeling better already for knowing that I wouldn't have to cycle thirty or so miles on a hot August day. "Have a lovely time, and tell the others I'll be all right this evening. Where are you going, by the way?"

"We're going to Gainsborough Hall which is a large Tudor house - English Heritage, I believe. Such a shame because you would've loved it - right up your street."

"Never mind. Take some pictures for me - that will do. Give my love to everyone. I'll wait here for Phil."

There was one place I wanted to visit in Lincoln, and by the time Phil turned up I'd formed a little plan in my head. "I wonder if we could take a taxi to the Usher Gallery. It's too far for me to walk."

"What a good idea! Come on, let's help you downstairs. It's nearly check-out time."

So that's how we spent the morning, very slowly walking arm in arm round the gallery, enjoying its hushed atmosphere and admiring all the paintings of Lincoln past and present by such masters as Peter da Wint and JMW Turner as well as the later work of LS Lowry and Toby Ward. I wouldn't have missed that morning for the world and with Phil as my strong right arm, I began to feel human again.

He called up a taxi which took us to a café where we each had a bowl of soup. "I've spoken to my mum, and she's happy to accommodate you and Don as well as me and Rosie. The others all have accommodation arranged nearby, but we've cancelled yours so that you can stay with us. She's a funny old thing, my mum, and seems stern and strict at first meeting but really she has a heart of gold. I told her a bit about your health problem and she's offered to give you healing."

"What do you mean, healing? I don't really expect to be healed at this stage of things."

"Perhaps not. But she is a healer and I think will be able to help you cope with what's coming."

"I see. Let me think about it. I'd like to meet her first."

"Yes, of course, I understand that."

It was time to go for our train and Phil was brilliant at organising the heavy electric bikes and the panniers and the backpacks because I still wasn't up to much. It was a funny one-carriage train to Grimsby. I don't think I've ever been on such a tiny train before but it was packed with, I assumed, Grimsby holidaymakers: lots of kids and mums and dads dressed for the beach, all with happy smiling faces. It was just fun looking around and listening to their conversations. I was having a great day!

The journey retraced our bicycle ride of a few days ago as it passed through Market Rasen and arrived at Barnetby le Wold where we had to change. Strange to be back here so soon. As we waited for the Manchester train which would take us to Scunthorpe, I could even see our Bed and Breakfast place in the High Street opposite the little supermarket.

It was restful on the platform in the afternoon sunshine. I needed that. A profusion of purple and white buddleias near the sidings were attracting dozens of butterflies. The clouds were high, flat islands in a sea of blue, barely moving on this breathless day. There were slight buzzing noises, either from electric wires or from little insects, I couldn't tell. Two middle-aged men sat on the platform bench, one hunched over his copy of the *Daily Mail*, the other leaning back and enjoying the full glare of the sun on his face. Two other men further up the platform, holding maps, remained in deep conversation for at least half an hour, and even when the train arrived, they took little notice of it. Three people alighted, and four people including us climbed on - but the two men stayed where they were, discussing their maps.

We passed through fields of maize, wheat and barley, but the rural scene began to give way to the industrial outskirts of Scunthorpe, where gantries, cranes, pipes, turbines and masts gradually came into view amidst scruffy bits of scrubland, pink with willowherb but mainly messy patches of grass and weed. A large sign said SAVE OUR STEEL, which reminded me of the importance of industry as well as agriculture to the Lincolnshire economy.

"So, are you going to manage a six-mile ride?" asked Phil.

"I think so. It's a beautiful afternoon, I'm feeling a lot better, and I'm looking forward to it."

In fact, it was what I had been hoping for all week: a long pull-up out of the town and we were soon freewheeling through the open countryside, where wind turbines dotted the distant horizon, and close by were fields full of sunflowers soaking up the heat of the late afternoon. All around was harvesting activity, and I could hardly keep my eyes off the tractors and balers sending clouds of dust into the air. As the shadows lengthened, long dark shapes flung themselves across the fields and hedgerows. I had to make sudden stops to admire the scenes which unfolded before my eyes, remembering to take a picture or two so that I could share my afternoon with the others.

At 5:00 o'clock we arrived in the village of Winterton and were soon inside Phil's mother's tiny listed cottage in King Street. Her name was Jean. "Come in, dear, and let me see you. Are you the one I'm healing? Yes, you are, I can tell. Come in, come in, and sit ye down here."

She was as thin as a rake, all skin and bone, tottering on her legs and wearing an old-fashioned floral summer dress. Her thin grey hair was tied back in a bun and her eyes were bright blue, just like Phil's. Her speech was soft and gentle, with a slight lilt, and I knew at once that whatever she did to me would only make me feel better.

"Let's have the healing now before the others come and there's a lot of kerfuffle. Lie down here, sweetheart, and I'll cover you up. There now. Close your eyes, relax and above all keep breathing! Leave the rest to me."

Oh, what bliss! I don't quite know what she did, but it was the most wonderful experience of my life. She didn't seem to touch me, but I knew she was there and I think her hands were floating over me. I have never felt so taken care of in my life and I didn't want it to end. Did I drift off to sleep? I'm not sure, but when the time came she said simply, "There now. All done. How do you feel?"

"Oh, that was wonderful. Thank you so much."

"I haven't really done very much, you know, but I have channelled some energy for you. I can't cure you, you know that, but I can help you get through it, so I suggest you come again next week." She stopped and turned round. "We've finished, Philip, so will you put the kettle on?"

We drank Earl Grey tea with lemon and ate one dry biscuit each. I wish I could tell you everything she told us about village life, and the birds in her garden, and the hedgehog which she feeds every evening, and the best places for blackberry-picking. She never stopped talking, and I thought to myself, "What an amazing woman, and what a life! Why doesn't Judith write a book about her?"

But I must continue with the story as there's still so much to tell. By early evening everyone had found their accommodation, and soon we were making our way in our hosts' cars to the village of Alkborough to see the grass maze known as Julian's Bower.

When we arrived the sun was low in the sky, sending dazzling rays across the confluence of three rivers, the Trent, the Ouse and the Humber. On the far horizon and in silhouette were the vast towers of Drax power station as well as more wind turbines. What a place of energy this was! Wind, sun, water, air and light - and all these within the view of this curious medieval grass maze, possibly created by monks from Walcot in Elizabethan times as a pathway to heaven. But just as possibly a place for children to play in.

"This will do very well," said Judith, who was standing next to me. "Maze number two, and I can now complete my poem. May I go last, please, Margot? I promise it will be ready by the final evening."

We returned to the village of Winterton where Phil had organised a simple cold buffet for us to share at his mother's house. She'd made delicious cold lemonade, and we tucked into all the goodies on the table. We shared the experiences of our day and I heard all about their ride and visit to Gainsborough House which apparently was wonderful.

"So I have missed the giant at Market Weighton, and now I have missed an English Heritage Tudor house. But on the other hand I have enjoyed the Usher Gallery in Lincoln, I have seen the steelworks of Scunthorpe, I have witnessed tractors and balers at work in the fields, I have seen dust clouds scudding across the Lincolnshire Wolds, and I have received healing from this wonderful lady. So I don't think I have missed anything."

"Talking of healing," Jean said, " I believe there's someone else here I need to treat."

"Who's that?" somebody asked.

There was silence in the room as Jean put down her plate and peered at each of us in turn.

"I think it's you, dear," she said, looking towards David.

"Why me?" he said, going bright red.

"Has some terrible tragedy happened to you recently?" she asked quietly.

"Oh, you mean my parents."

"Possibly. Tell me about it."

There was a sudden hush in the room because we'd never spoken openly about the awful circumstances of his parents' death, as if it was a taboo subject. But now David was being put on the spot and he was clearly feeling uncomfortable. "The fact was, my mum and dad were shot dead in a terrorist shooting in Tunisia last year."

There was an intake of breath at the enormity of it, and Jean closed her eyes. "Is that the truth, then?" she asked quietly.

"Yes," David replied with a tone of slight indignation, "Of course it is."

"I'm not so sure," she said, almost pianissimo, and then remained silent.

David looked at James, but James was looking down at the ground, not able to give his partner the support he wanted. But after a few moments, James looked up. "You'd better say, David. It's now or never."

Everyone stared at David who had now gone pale. Jean came to the rescue. "They weren't your parents, were they?"

David couldn't bring himself to say yes or no - but instead, looking at Jean, asked, "Can you give me healing, please?"

Jean led David upstairs, and we turned to James.

"You've probably realised by now that David was adopted as a child," he said, "and it's troubled him all his life. He only told me years after I came to know him, in fact when we formed our relationship. I think he feels it's a stigma which he carries round with him - you know, the thought that he was rejected - and for years he had a terrible inferiority complex."

"Has he ever made enquiries about his parents?" I asked.

"No, never. His adoptive parents gave him a wonderful home and upbringing, so it was a big shock when he found out. Since they died in such tragic circumstances, he felt life had given him another huge blow, and he's been having counselling. But healing will be good for him, too."

I know Phil wanted to recite his poem in his old family house, so after a few minutes pause I said, "It's getting late now, but let's hear Phil's story. I think you call it a ballad, is that right?"

"Yes. It's based on a dream I had, which I quickly scribbled down, and when I woke up it was complete gobbledygook, but I thought, well, heck, there's a story in here somewhere, so here it is."

"But first, my little introduction, please:

Phil the builder, joiner, painter, plast'rer
Of all such trades he surely was the master,
Grizzled, wrinkled, but with twinkling eye,
A ready wit and never a grievous sigh.
Firm and steady, loyal as a rock,
Calm, impassive, nothing could him shock."

"Hmm, I'm not sure about that, Margot - makes me sound like an old fossil! Anyway, here goes."

The Ballad of Adam Goodapple

I dreamt last night of Adam: a barrow boy was he.
He'd had enough of London town and longed to go to sea.
He lacked the cash to buy a boat and fit it with a crew.
How was he to make enough? He really had no clue.

One day at school he learnt about a tale from ancient Greece,
Concerning Jason, the Argonauts, and a magic Golden Fleece.
He longed to navigate the world in search of buried treasure.
A fortune-hunting mariner! - his idea of perfect pleasure.

Another day he learnt about the Greek Hesperides,
Evening nymphs, otherwise called the Atlantides.
They guarded golden apples in a garden far away -
"The western corner of the world," he heard his teacher say.

When it came to apples Adam knew a thing or two,
But apples made of solid gold - could that really be true?
"On seeking out these apples my future does depend.
What's furthest west? I have it! I'll journey to Land's End!"

Now of his future destiny Adam had strong feelings
That his name, Goodapple, meant more than apple-peelings.
For him the fruit was bound up with a future most auspicious
And what could be more fruitful than a true Golden Delicious?

Early on the morrow he packed spare sock and shoe,
Tied them to the end of a stick which over his shoulder he threw.
Nothing could be simpler. His crew would appear on the way,
Like-minded folk in search of some fun - "Join me, tag along," he'd say.

Quite soon he met a little girl, looking bored and tired.
"I'm Adam." "And I'm Lily, hoping to be inspired."
"Will you join me on my quest, be a member of my crew?
If so, what part is best for you - I mean, what can you do?"

"I could be First Mate on board your sturdy ship.
I'll keep control as we rock and roll on our wavy ocean trip.
I'd love to come, be part of the fun and join your gallant crew,
I'll dance and sing and play the flute - and I can cook a stew!"

Adam walked on with Lily, the day was fine and bright,
The air quite still as they climbed a hill, drawn by a curious sight:
A lonely man with a telescope was peering at the moon
Fading quickly in the western sky, disappearing soon.

"Will you join my growing band?" asked Adam of this gent.
"We're heading west where life is best - a sort of experiment!"
"I'll join you, of course! And with my 'scope I'll navigate the way
By the light of the stars, Venus and Mars. Simply call me Ray."

Ahead of them they saw a bus, but the driver was a villain.
"He's hijacked us!" the people cried. "Where are we being driven?"
A cowboy came on horseback swirling a big lasso:
"Don't worry, folks. Hold on tight! I'm here to rescue you."

Twirling his rope he launched it and, sailing through the air,
It wrapped round the bus without any fuss. "Our hero, we declare!"
The villain was roundly admonished. "I'm sorry. What can I do
To make amends for my wicked ways?" "You can come and join our crew,"

Said Adam, "Sign up to our party, join this quest
In search of the apples which gleam in the west -
And as for your duty, this much I can say:
Keep hijacking pirates well out of our way!"

The four agreed most heartily, shaking hands on this and that.
"We're Adam, Ray and Lily. You?" "My name is Matt.
"I'm hoping with your influence to kick my life of crime."
"No doubt of that!" laughed Adam. "Your future looks sublime!"

My dream now led me to a rock beside a sylvan lake
On which there sat a princess bemoaning her mistake.
"I've lost my realm, my husband, my children and my way -
Someone take me to my grave and there my head I'll lay."

Discovering a princess in this wretched situation,
They listened and consoled her for her piteous condition.
Then Adam said, "I know it's hard but try to look ahead.
Please join us on our voyage to places new instead."

The princess wiped her tears and said, "Enough I've cried.
You're right, there is no turning back. I know, because I've tried.
May I join you in your venture to find treasure in the west,
Buy a ship and sail away? This is my fond request!"

They travelled on together through sunshine and through rain,
Slept in barns, on haystacks and once on Salisbury Plain.
Passers-by would greet them, asking, "Where to are you heading?"
Some fed them soup and sandwiches, others offered bedding.

Among themselves they told their tales, which oftentimes were cruel:
Lily had no parents, Adam was bullied at school,
Matt had mixed with criminals, Ray had no close friends,
While the princess wept for her mistake, unable to make amends.

But sharing can be bonding, and their friendship grew apace -
Sadness yields to happiness - smiles grew on every face.
Through Somerset and Devon and Cornwall they progressed
Till Ray announced: "I see Land's End, the point that's furthest west!"

But what a disappointment! No tree there could be seen,
No bush, no twig, no apples either golden, red or green.
Of vegetation, not a sign - just endless rock and sea.
"I'm speechless," Adam whispered. "How can you forgive me?

"I've not fulfilled my promise, Ray, of navigation by the stars,
And, Lily, no opportunity to entertain us tars -
Matt, my pal, you've been denied the chance to make that break,
And for you, Princess, no foreign shores to forget your grave mistake."

Adam, inconsolable, sat down upon a tuft
Of withered grass, where he cried and sniffed and snuffed.
The air was still, the sun shone down, so pleasant was the day,
Yet this poor boy could not rejoice, so deep was his dismay.

They formed a circle on the ground
And listened to the wailing sound
Of seagulls cawing overhead,
White-breasted mourners of the dead.

At last the Princess broke the spell:
"Dear Adam, you have done so well!
You've given us such great relief,
Each speaking of our personal grief.

"Now understand how things transpire,
Like a phoenix from a fire.
While you've been leading us along,
Piping a tune, singing a song,

"Matters very near the heart
Have blossomed from a bud-like start.
Let me explain my meaning clearly,
We've discovered what we cherish dearly!

"Lily, as honest as the day,
Lacks a parent to lead the way,
While Matt, transformed by her example,
Will step into a role paternal.

"And as for me, my life's turned round,
Because my darling Ray I've found.
The past is now a distant land -
Forward we'll go, hand in hand.

"So you see, dear Adam, no riches, no wealth,
But a much greater treasure: happiness, health!
No golden apples at our journey's end
But in you we have found a most precious friend."

Adam looked at Lily twirling round and round,
Floating in the breeze, skirting o'er the ground -
Matt was doing handstands with a youthful grace,
The years now lifted from his brow, lines falling from his face.

Ray also looked much younger as he bowed to his princess:
"Will you marry me, my sweetheart, thus ending my distress?"
She took his hand and kissed it: "I'm truly yours, my love.
Together we will walk life's path, blessed by the stars above."

"Although great joy has resulted," said Adam, "from this trip,
Still I am quite penniless and can't afford a ship.
I'd set my hopes upon a voyage for glory, fun and fame,
But now I've reached this rocky point, everything's much the same."

The others' hearts went out to him, aware of his dismay,
Their hopes fulfilled, their dreams come true, but his so far away.
They walked down to the water's edge to watch the setting sun:
Its golden beams were dazzling - the day's course nearly run.

But as they watched together, they heard the strangest sound
Like a foghorn in the distance, yet there was no fog around.
Looking north they saw a sight which took their breath away -
A glorious ship with billowing sails gliding smoothly across the bay.

"We're calling you, Goodapple," they heard the captain shout,
"If it's voyaging you want, I'm prepared to try you out."
"How did you hear about me?" "A cowboy on a horse
Knew of your hopes and told us. Remember him?" "Of course!"

Adam, turning to his friends, exclaimed, "My dream's come true!
You've brought me luck, Princess and Ray, and Matt, and Lily, too!"
They laughed and hugged and waved farewell - soon Adam was aboard
Anticipating every thrill this great life can afford.

And as the ship sailed t'wards the sun, I woke. All visions fled,
The sea, the sky, the five dear friends... and here I was in bed!
The dream stayed with me long enough to write it down in time:
The Ballad of Adam Goodapple now immortalised in rhyme!

We gave Phil a round of applause for his delightful and crazy poem which had lifted our spirits and dispelled any feelings of disharmony from earlier.

"Poor David!" I whispered to Don.

"Well maybe, yes" he replied, "but I'm sure he will be feeling better now, thanks to Jean. Bedtime now."

Wednesday

I woke to the tinkling sound of a teacup. Don was still in his pyjamas but had been downstairs to make my early morning cuppa. He was drawing the curtains and letting in a stream of sunlight. Hearing me stir, he turned and smiled, then came and sat next to me on the edge of the bed. "How are you feeling, love?"

I wiggled myself about under the sheets and gave his question a moment's thought. But you always know when you're well, don't you, and have had a good sleep. "You know, I think I'm fine – absolutely fine. Isn't that wonderful! So, tell me what's happening today? Where are we, and where are we going?"

He fetched a map as I propped myself up against a pillow, climbed back into bed and we spread it out on the duvet.

"We are here," he said, pointing to Winterton. He then traced his finger roughly north to the Humber River, then east through South Ferriby to the Humber Bridge, north across the bridge then west through North Ferriby.

"We will pick up cycle route number 65 for the rest of the ride until we arrive in Howden, which is where we're going to spend the night."

I have to say it all looked pretty boring, flat and featureless on the map but so what? I put my arm round his shoulder, kissed him on the cheek and said, "Perfect, love, absolutely perfect."

I showered, rubbed myself all over with a big fluffy towel and put on my last set of clean clothes, feeling strangely light. I had eaten so little yesterday that it was partly a weight thing, and when I weighed myself on the scales I uttered a little whoop of joy - a rare event! Gosh, I couldn't wait to be on my bicycle again - and that's a pretty rare event, too.

There was tea and toast for breakfast, as well as some fruit salad left over from last night's dinner. Phil, Rosie, Don and I sat around the table while Jean, who didn't eat breakfast, hovered around topping up our tea and toasting bread.

She told me quite sternly not to overdo it today. "You should really be resting, but I know you must carry on. Please try to be sensible, drink plenty of water and take as many breaks as you need to. It's going to be a long hot day."

Don booked another appointment for healing in a week's time. We shook hands (she was not the hugging type), and thanked her for a wonderful stay. She watched us at her front door while we loaded up our bikes and put on our helmets. Gradually the others arrived so that we could all set off together. She looked so small and frail on the doorstep wearing her neat little apron, but in fact she was a very strong lady.

"Thanks, mum," said Phil, giving her a peck on her cheek. But she was more interested now in David. "I'm here if you need me, but I don't think you will. You did what you had to, and that was good. Now, go on your way, everyone, and have a lovely ride."

As we set off, she gave us a little wave and disappeared indoors.

We cycled into bright sunshine and, as I had lost my dark glasses, I had to keep my head well down to avoid being blinded. I had this urge to talk to everyone today, because I had missed their company on yesterday's ride and now wanted to make up for it. It was just a matter of cycling up next to Peter, then Angus, Judith, then Cynthia, and exchanging a few words, finding out how they were and assuring them that I was fine again.

Crossing back over the Humber Bridge was quite different this time because there wasn't a breath of wind, there were no other cyclists and the water was still beneath us. Its surface was covered in swirling patterns of oily currents which looked translucent in the morning light.

Once across the bridge we headed west to North Ferriby until we found ourselves on the outskirts of the village of Brough. There we stopped at a Morrisons for coffee and croissants. I shared a table with Winnie, James and Tammy and I heard more about their cycle ride yesterday as well as their overnight accommodation in Winterton. Oh, I wished today would last forever!

Back on our bikes, we now left the busy roads and the route turned into a rough track. The sky was a light blue, the clouds were high and thin, the air was warm. This was rural South Yorkshire on a hot late August morning and we took it steadily to savour every moment: fields of sunflowers, harvested bales either lying singly in the fields or stacked in precarious towers, farmyards, ripening chestnut trees, morning glories in the hedgerows. There was a farmhouse which had products for sale and a small blackboard with the writing: *Baking by Hannah, jam tarts two for a pound, proceeds for Macmillan, all pots and baskets now £3.50.* Further on two tractors were pulling vast loads of straw bales. We followed them into the farmyard, rather cheekily, and took photos as they upended the trucks, spilling out the contents, which tumbled onto a piece of spare ground near the barns.

On and on we went, until we arrived at Market Weighton Lock. Two other cyclists were coming the other way and we stopped to have a chat.

"We started this morning in Chesterfield, and we're heading for the coast."

My, oh my, what a distance! It made me tired to think about it and immediately I knew I had to rest. We had bought sandwiches, crisps and drinks at Morrisons, so this seemed a good place for a picnic. We were beside the Humber River and could either look south across the water or north up the canal towards that scene of endless rain last Friday. It seemed such a long time ago now!

"What about a Lincolnshire Tale at this point?" asked Rosie. Good idea! Whose turn was it?

"I think this would be a good place for mine," said Winnie, rummaging in her rucksack for her poem. While she looked I read out the following lines:

There was a lady lived in Wales called Winnie,
Preferred the countryside to any city.
For long she'd worked the land, she'd planted trees,
Collected honey from her hives of bees,
Sold vegetables and flowers to her neighbours.
So admirable to live by her own labours!

"Thanks, Margot. This is an outdoor kind of poem, so it's suitable for today and this situation. It's a bit long, I'm afraid so make sure you're all comfortable and relaxed. I hope you like it."

The Song of Gaia, the earth goddess

In the beginning was the world,
Peaceful, calm and still,
For long remaining silent,
Its purpose to fulfil.

"Let's create some liveliness,"
To herself she said one day.
"Birds, people, insects, animals –
Come out and have a play!"

The grey dawn broke, the sun was dim,
Strange life forms, stretching every limb,
Appeared, confused, within the sea:
"What name are you? Who might I be?"

Emerging from the blue green soup,
Huddling together in a group,
They felt a bond between each one –
"Let's keep together and have some fun!

"Come, hurry all, who tarry below,
Let's swim into life's onward flow.
The moon is rising with gentle light,
Revealing a land of great delight."

Escaping to the world above
They felt a special bond of love.
"Here's a place where friends can live
In harmony, to share and give."

They gathered on a sandy shore.
"This Paradise we will explore
And make a home where we will strive
To live in peace so we can thrive."

Jumping for joy, they admired the scene
Of golden meadows and fields of green,
Hillsides adorned with abundant trees,
Waving their branches in the breeze.

In cooling showers or pleasant heat,
Desires grew – they stamped their feet,
Became excited, inflamed by passion,
Cavorted in unseemly fashion.

An angel passing overhead
Looked down upon the merriment
Of humans tweeting like silly birds.
She flew down close to hear their words.

"This world is abundant with fabulous wealth
And it's ours for the taking - it's all for ourself!
We'll feast and make merry as never before.
Let's take what we want – and then take some more!"

These foolish words she heard with pain,
Decided no longer to remain
But hurried back to her relations:
"I'll make a report and have consultations."

The angels listened with growing concern.
"These humans clearly have much to learn.
Tell them the legend of the goddess Gaia
Who took revenge in flood and fire,

"How people suffered a dismal fate.
Don't worry if you exaggerate!
It's vital to give them a solemn warning.
No time to waste. Tomorrow morning!"

When dawn arose she flew on wings
Of silvery white and silken strings,
And found the people in ignorant chat,
"I will have this – you can have that."

She interrupted with smiling face,
"A natural law governs this place.
Think of yourselves as guardians, not keepers.
Your role's one of service – not of self-seekers.

"If you infringe this basic trust,
You'll be dismissed, returned to dust,
This Paradise be forced to leave,
No further chance will you receive.

"Let me relate what happened before:
A previous race broke the law,
They stole and destroyed Gaia's wealth,
Wasted resources, ruined her health.

"Ravaged and poisoned, her balance upset,
Climatic extremes – too hot – too wet –
Icebergs melted – oceans grew higher –
The goddess shook angrily in flood and fire.

" 'What have we done?' they cried out in vain,
'This land is parched – but here's endless rain.'
'Where forests once grew, it's now barren plain.'
'Where once grew green fields, a black ugly stain!'

"Woefully crying in sheer desperation,
But the damage was done – there was no reparation.
Destruction was rife, and they cowered in terror,
Knew they would pay for their dismal error.

"Weeping and wailing, they paid the full price:
In miserable sorrow they lost Paradise.
Expelled from the world of earthly delight,
Thrust into darkness, excluded from light.

"Many millennia passed before Gaia
Recovered her balance, renewed her desire
To people her planet with those who love peace
And justice and freedom." Thus did she speak.

A breathtaking pause, then one broke the spell:
"Did this really happen, this story you tell?"
"A legend, let's call it," the angel replied,
"A story to learn from, with a warning inside.

"So bearing in mind where wantonness led,
Make sure on this earth that lightly you tread.
In harmony with Gaia, the goddess to please,
You will live happily in comfort and ease.

"Take care of the animals, the birds and the bees,
The cat and the rabbit, the owl - oh, and please
Keep clear of all litter the beaches, the seas,
And then above all plant plenty of trees.

"The tortoise, the fox are entrusted to you
As are the deserts, and the skies deeply blue.
Of the wonders of nature these are only a few -
Even so, remember to give them their due.

"We angels respond when we see that you care
By a loving embrace and a touch light as air.
Whenever you act to keep the earth fair
We smile and rejoice with hearts debonair."

The angel had finished, she floated away.
"It's now up to us," the people did say.
"The sky's multicoloured, hills emerald green -
That's how it should stay: a picturesque scene."

xxx

Let's begin to feel deeply a sense of belonging,
Knowing the earth as an ever-evolving
Constantly changing animate being -
A new way of living, a new way of seeing.

Feel the roar of the sea, feel the light of the moon,
Feel the wind and the rain playing their tune,
Then in service to Gaia we'll know we belong
To this living world. And so ends my song.

Well, of course we liked it – who wouldn't? She'd read it very slowly so it had a somewhat hypnotic effect. Like the day, and like this cycle ride itself, I wish it could have gone on forever. There was a great reluctance to move on but eventually we did - and our bumpy rough track continued, along a road lined with poplars, beside a field edged with a few uncut ears of corn, a house where gladioli were peeping up through a fence of iron railings, straw stacks piled as if to create a replica of Stonehenge, verges still colourful with wildflowers, and now a signpost indicating only two miles to Howden. Oh dear, journey's end in sight.

But then, best and most wonderful surprise of all, at the last gasp of our ride, we pulled in at the opening to a field, drawn by the sound of a massive red combine harvester. We were mesmerised by its vast blades and the sight of the sparkling grain flying in the sunlight, creating clouds of glittering dust. We must have stood there for ten minutes watching the vast beast move up and down the field, threshing and cutting, lifting and lowering its circling blades, harvesting its crop.

By now we had been exchanging waves with the driver, and he must have been amused by our funny antics with phones - how ridiculous we must have looked! Anyone would think there was something novel about harvesting a field. One final wave and we were on our way - but to me it was the highlight of the trip.

We cycled into Howden, found our accommodation and I collapsed into bed.

"Enjoy the rest of the day," I called out to Don from beneath the sheets. "Take lots of photos, and tell me what I missed later."

And I slept and slept.

xxx

Winnie and Peter had a large gathering around them at the bar before dinner when Don and I came down at about 6:00 o'clock.

"Oh good, they're here now so we'll tell you what happened," said Peter. "Unlike the rest of you, who've been exploring all afternoon, we've been sorting out the troubles of one very unhappy landlord."

"That's not entirely true," said Winnie, "but that I suppose was the gist of it. We arrived at our bed and breakfast place which is between the town and the station. It's a big house set well back from the road, and has quite a large garden, with outside kennels and a small paddock where we saw two horses grazing. Anyway, we rolled up, rang the doorbell and the owner answered, looking very flustered.

'I'm sorry,' he said - his name was Bill Craddock by the way - 'but I've been getting my knickers in a twist - excuse the expression - over the bookings, and I'm not sure I can accommodate you.'

"It turned out, when we looked at his book, that he had muddled us up with another couple called Unwin, who were down to come this time next week. He told us that since his wife passed away in the spring, he hadn't been coping very well and was seriously contemplating selling up. You can imagine where this is leading. Peter and I immediately became interested and we spent the rest of the afternoon discussing the possibility of us taking it over."

"It had everything we could possibly want," added Peter, "and it would be doing him a good turn too."

"It's near a town, near the railway station, and has as much land as we could manage..."

"...and great walking country for the dogs."

"...and a paddock for that horse which the girls have always wanted."

"The only question remaining is what to do with Henry."

"For all we know he might have Angela back by now and if so then they'll be wanting a place of their own."

We all expressed our happiness for them and of course I was particularly pleased that Don's dear old university friend, Peter, would be back nearby. It was really no distance from York to Howden, and I could just imagine them becoming drinking partners again after all these years. That is, if Winnie didn't mind too much!

So it was quite appropriate that Peter had the final word that evening after supper with his poem. Here is my prologue:

Of Peter I would say 'gregarious,
Jokey, chatty, happy – nervy too.'
He started cycling holidays for us
So to him a truly massive debt is due.
Best friend from student days in Durham city,
Annoying, cheeky, teasing, always witty,
An extra rhyming couplet is yours
For cycle rides through Dales and Wolds and Moors.

"Yes, well, thank you, Margot. Quite accurate, I guess. Here is my poem, which is of course about a dog. Hope you like it."

The Ballad of Sam, the Alsatian

This tale began in Settle town
Amid the Yorkshire Dales.
It could have happened anywhere,
In Scotland, Ireland, Wales,
In China or Australia,
Peru or the Seychelles,
Wherever dogs sense failure -
This happened in the Dales.

Sam's what you'd call a rescue dog,
An orphan, you might say,
A handsome boy, pure Alsatian,
But what a final destination!
Unowned, unloved, nowhere to play,
Chained to a kennel like a log,
He slept by night and barked by day -
It shouldn't happen to a dog.

Others in this situation
Didn't seem to feel frustration,
But Sam was made to question things:
"A wholesome life is one that <u>sings!</u>
We eat and sleep, then have a walk,
Then eat and sleep some more.
I need to run, and have some fun
Like scrapping paw to paw!

"Fighting for food's not my idea
Of fun - it's bare existence.
I need to get away from here -
Put it at safe distance.
I have in mind a gipsy life,
And if that means I'm shiv'ring
In wind and wet and snow and ice,
At least I would be living!"

That night he had the strangest dream
Of rocks and lakes and mountains -
Birds flying high, fish in the streams,
And sparkling crystal fountains.
All nature seemed to beckon him:
"Join our adventurous life!
We work and play together
In times of joy and strife."

He woke to feel surrounded by
A blanket of protection.
With mighty strain he broke his chain
Then said, "Now, which direction?"
At once arose a gentle wind
Which whispered in his ear:
"Follow the path towards the sun;
Good fortune will appear."

He had no doubts - he bounded out
Of the yard where he'd been held.
Happy was he at last to be free,
All trace of sadness dispelled.
Said the fields and the fences: "Keep on, keep on!"
And the trees by the track the same:
"Make the most of your freedom! We're trapped in our treedom,
But for you now the world is aflame!"

Feeling alive for the very first time
Young Sam felt the blood in his veins
Boiling and surging, everything merging
In the life-force that Nature sustains.
"At last I am free! This is true liberty
To feel happy as never before.
Hills, rivers and trees - even my fleas! -
I love you as never before!"

The track led him on through a sun-dappled glade
Where the leaves cried, "Somebody's calling!
We fear a boy's drowning, so do not delay,
Or the outcome could be appalling!"
Sam doubled his speed - his response to this need
Gave him a wonderful feeling:
A mixture of courage and infinite strength
And a purpose which made life worth living.

At the foot of the hill was a flood, like a lake,
And a ford where two brothers were playing.
But one had slipped in by a silly mistake,
And the other was calling and praying:
"Is anyone there? Come quick, I need help
To rescue my brother from drowning."
Sam heard the boy's call, and emitting a yelp
Sprang down the hill, leaping and bounding.

The boy was immersed in the water's cold grip
And his boots were stuck fast in the mud.
The other was pulling with all of his strength,
Overwhelmed by the force of the flood.
Sam dived in deep, took all the boy's weight
On his back, without any falter,
And slowly at last, released from the grasp
Of the mud, he crawled out of the water.

"Oh, what an escape! I thought that my fate
Was bound up in the rushes and reeds
Of this silly lake. By the way, my name's Jake.
Thank God you sprang out of the trees!
I really must thank you for letting me climb
Onto your body, when all seemed so black!
You came to the rescue at just the right time.
What's your name, boy?" while stroking his back.

"It's Sam," said the other (his name was Mike),
"It says on his collar - you see?
But who is your master?" At this the dog whined
As if to say, "Can you take me?"
"I reckon he's homeless," said Jake. "That's no problem.
We'll give you a home, don't you worry.
Mum and Dad will be grateful, they'll give you a plateful
Of food when we tell them our story."

My tale's nearly over: boy and dog are both clean,
The mud washed completely away,
Their parents relieved but can scarcely believe
The story the boys have to say.
They sit in the garden, the sunshine pours down
Drying Jake's clothes and Sam's coat.
The dog has a home, but the best thing of all:
Jake has Sam - on whom he can dote.

Very sweet and Peterish. We wished each other goodnight, exchanged a few hugs and trotted off to bed.

Thursday

Another bad night, a really bad one, and in the morning I knew I couldn't go on. "I'm sorry, love, but you're going to have to take me home."

"That's fine, darling. When you're ready to get up, I'll order a taxi for the station, and we'll go back together. You've done really well, only missing one day. As soon as we're back, I'll ring for a doctor and..."

"No, absolutely not," I said firmly. "If you ring for a doctor, I know what they'll do: they'll drag me into hospital and I won't come out again. All I want is to go home and then straight to bed for the rest of the day. Hopefully I'll be all right for our farewell dinner."

"But..."

"But me no buts. I absolutely insist. You can do anything you like with me after that, I shan't mind a bit. I'll be a good girl and make no objections. But I want to see this through to the end because...well, it's going to be wonderful."

I didn't want to see the others so Don went and told them what was happening, and that I wished them all a lovely journey back through Selby - another place I will have missed - and then the satellite route - that, too - but I was becoming used to this now. James came and helped with bags, cycled my bike to the station, and somehow found his way back to Howden where he joined the others after breakfast for their departure.

I dragged myself out of bed at about midday, Don put me in a taxi, cycled straight to the station, and within an hour we were on the train to York. Not exactly my plan for *Cycling with Margot* but still. Sensing I was close to tears as I stared out at the fields which I would probably never cycle through again, Don held my hand tightly.

But it was funny stopping in Selby, for it was horseracing at the Knavesmire this week, and on piled the racing punters, smart young men wearing their outfits of shiny grey suits, pink shirts and satin ties, and the younger ones in their snappy waistcoats arm in arm with a dolly bird wearing an extravagant hat, and impossible shoes only good for tottering. Don and I couldn't help laughing at one pair which was winged with golden feathers above the two-inch heel, as if she hoped they would make her fly.

In complete contrast, a somewhat overweight young man, with untidy brown hair and straggly beard, alighted, pushing a sort of shaded pram, but instead of a baby, there was a panting King Charles Spaniel.

"It's a pet-stroller," he said. "Poor old boy, he's got heart disease, and is completely blind. Aren't you, poppet?" and he gave him a stroke.

"Where are you taking him?" I asked.

"We're visiting my mum's in Scarborough. He likes to play in the waves - don't you?" and there was more stroking.

I was amused by his T-shirt: two horses, one saying to the other: "Look at me. I'm a pretty unicorn." "No, you're not, Barry. You've just stuck a twig on your head with duct tape."

Once at York, Don padlocked the bikes in the station forecourt, then helped me to a taxi. I was feeling utterly helpless, and I was concerned about him having to take me home, then return for one bike, then return for the other. And how would he manage all the luggage? Poor lamb!

Fortunately I slept all afternoon, which made up for last night, and by six o'clock I was ready for a bath and some clean clothes. In fact, it was fun to choose something from my wardrobe, and polish my nails and put on some mascara. I would be the Belle of the Ball!

We arrived at the hotel as fresh as daisies, while the others drifted in, dripping with sweat and dust. They quickly had their showers and tidied up so we were all in the bar by 7:00. I wanted to know all about their day, and they all wanted to know about mine as well as how I was feeling. As soon as I started sipping on a glass of dry sherry, I found I even had a little appetite for some crisps and a nut or two.

So we were all sitting down in groups of four at square tables, when there was the sound of a gong. Henry had appeared at the bar with Angela, and he was all smiles, banging away at the gong for all he was worth.

"Stop it, Henry!" she exclaimed. "Everyone's looking at you. How embarrassing!"

Angela was looking so pretty in a long brown and white dress, with her silver hair curled around her face framing her dimpled cheeks and pale grey eyes. She could only have been five foot four or five, and looked tiny next to Henry's somewhat gangling form, but you could tell already they were a couple again. They came over to us, arm in arm.

"How have you all been?" he asked. "How are you, Margot? Did you all see Julian's Bower? Isn't it wonderful? Yes, please, Phil, just a half of lager. Oh, and what would you like, dear? Dubonnet and lemonade? Where shall we sit?"

Henry could not stop talking, but all the time he was being so solicitous towards Angela, finding a cushion for her back, and checking she wasn't sitting under any air-conditioning, " because she hates draughts, don't you, dear?"

It was all quite comical, but very sweet. And now we managed to put the tables together, and sat round them in one large group, because we were not the least bit interested in ourselves any more but only in the new couple. Angela made it clear she wanted to talk to us.

"I know what friends you all are, and Henry has been telling me everything about you over the last couple of days, so when he said he wanted to come to your final dinner, of course I wanted to come too, and try to explain a few things before the holiday was over and everyone went home."

She wasn't in the least overawed about talking to total strangers, and as she told her story I felt that she was making the most of the opportunity to unburden herself of some deeply held secrets which she had been hanging on to for far too long.

"I know what Henry has been telling you, and he even read out to me the poem which he composed. But I want to put the record straight, because what happened was by no means all his fault. Looking back, I was not in many ways a very good wife to him. I did not appreciate how good an artist he was, I was a very timid mousy little thing, set in my ways and with no spirit of adventure at all. I wouldn't even go to an Indian Restaurant with him! I was used to Lincoln and had my Cathedral and my bookshop, and my writing, and really that was all I wanted.

"So when he suggested uprooting and going to Scotland, well, it was like going to Timbuctoo! I couldn't bear the thought of it, but looking back I realise I was only thinking of myself, and not giving a moment's thought to what Henry needed in terms of advancing his career."

While she took a sip of her drink, Cynthia leant forward and asked her, "Tell us about your son."

"Now I come to the most appalling part of the whole story. As soon as Henry left, I went into a complete panic. I realised at once how completely dependent I had been on him all our married life, and now I felt completely at sea. I became more nervous than ever, and I had to take anti-depressants to calm myself down. But somehow these made me clumsy and forgetful, and I couldn't keep up with the paperwork connected with the gallery, and some days I even found it difficult to get up in the morning."

"But you had a child to look after," said Tammy. "How old was he by then?"

"He was five. Fortunately he was quiet and docile, a good little boy, but I was a gibbering wreck. My neighbours and friends knew I was in a bad way, and some of them did offer to help with shopping and cooking and so on. Anyway, it all came to a head one morning at breakfast, when a percolator of hot coffee fell from my hands and fell right onto David who was sitting on the floor beneath me in his pyjamas."

There was an audible gasp from everyone, not only from the enormity of what had happened but also from her use of the name 'David.'

"We all thought his name was Harry," I said in amazement.

"That was his second name – in fact it was Henry, after his father, which got shortened to Harry. I always preferred David but Henry here," nudging him with her elbow, "preferred Harry."

At this point we became aware of a certain bustle of whispering between James and David. I heard James say, "Go on, ask her," so David, tense and pale, looked up and asked, "Excuse me, Angela, but this is important. Was the boy badly scarred?"

"Yes, of course he was, dreadfully scarred right across his chest. He screamed and screamed, and I didn't know what to do. It was the most terrible accident and all I could think of doing was calling 999. Fortunately my neighbour, Joyce Dean, heard the sound of the boy's cries and came banging on the front door. I went downstairs and let her in, and she was wonderful. Joyce had been a nurse, you see, so when the ambulance arrived things were more or less under control. I was sitting in an armchair shaking, beside myself with worry and fear..."

This time James interrupted. "Angela, what happened to the boy?"

"He was taken into care. And so was I, at least by Joyce. She was wonderful to me. I don't know how long I stayed there, but she nursed me over a period of months and got me back on my feet again. But it was quite obvious I was in no state to look after David, so he was taken to an orphanage and then fostered out. I missed him dreadfully, of course, but I had to get myself sorted out and it took a long time. I really think if it hadn't been for Joyce I might have – well, it doesn't bear contemplating."

By now the same thought was going through everybody's minds. Nobody spoke, and the only sound was the piped music in the bar, the rustle of a newspaper from the gentleman in the far corner and a conversation between two ladies at another table. We were watching James and David conferring again.

"Angela, this is an old sort of question but was the scar on Harry's chest in any particular shape?"

"Yes, it was. I couldn't bring myself to go to the hospital, so Joyce reported on his progress to me and said how he would be perfectly all right in time, but he would have a scar for the rest of his life which bore an uncanny resemblance to the continent of Africa."

"My God! I would know that scar anywhere," exclaimed James. "In fact, I know it intimately. Show them, David."

"What, here?"

"Yes, don't be shy. It's important, David, to you, to everyone."

So with that David stood up and walked towards Angela and Henry, while undoing his shirt buttons. He knelt on the floor in front of them and revealed his bare chest. From where I was sitting a few chairs away I could see his scar which had the unmistakable shape of Africa.

"It's him!" exclaimed Angela. "It must be, our little David. Oh, my goodness!"

"This is like the ending of a Shakespeare comedy," laughed Angus, to which Cynthia added,

"Or like something from a Mozart opera. Do you remember that bit in *The Marriage of Figaro*?"

Peter picked up the theme and started singing very quietly from the Act Three sextet: "*Sua madre, sua madre...*"

"This is unbelievable," said Henry, clasping his forehead with his hands. "All these years I have known David, and yet all the time he has been my... my little Harry!"

"*Suo padre, suo padre...*"

But wasn't this all too unbelievable for words? There were so many unanswered questions hanging in the air: why hadn't she done this - or that - or the other? And was David really their son? Could it be verified? Where are the documents? What about a DNA test? But all these doubts and questions were completely drowned out by the sight of the happy threesome, and Cynthia shouting, "Hurrah!" and leading a round of applause which we all took up while the trio embraced and hugged each other. A waiter approached, looking slightly nonplussed by the sight of a bare-chested guest, but maintained sufficient decorum to announce calmly, "Your tables are ready, ladies and gentlemen."

"We'll need two more place settings, please," said Phil equally calmly.

"No problem, sir. Follow me."

XXX

After a more than usually lively dinner, in which it was decided that Angela and Henry would be moving to an attractive house in Beverley which was in need of occupiers, Peter and Winnie would definitely be selling their smallholding in Wales and moving to a bed and breakfast establishment in Howden, and Judith would be writing about a dysfunctional family in Lincoln which became functional again, I remembered that she had not yet told her Lincolnshire Tale which would round off the series.

"Are you ready?" I asked her.

"Yes, I have it here."

So I tapped on my wine glass, and when everyone was quiet, I gave my final little prologue:

Behold our Judith, novelist supreme,
Persisted and fulfilled her lifelong dream
Of publication with "The Golden Key,"
A tale of wit, romance and mystery.
And as our week brings end to all confusion,
So Judith brings my book to its conclusion.

"Okay, I'll do my best but this didn't work out at all as I hoped it would. My favourite poem is *The Rime of the Ancient Mariner* by Coleridge, and I wanted to write a kind of pastiche which would bring in some of the elements of our ride around Lincolnshire. Unfortunately it got totally out of hand and turned into something rather ridiculous. For what it's worth, here it is:

The Rime of the Ancient Cyclist

There was an ancient cyclist
And he stopped each passer-by.
"Have you seen my sweetheart?"
He asked them with a sigh.

They asked her name - "Katrina.
We met when we were four.
Many years have passed since then,
Journeys by the score."

"We met when we were infants
Near the brook by fields of rye,
And now I must regain her
In the days before I die."

"We haven't seen your sweetheart
In the forest dark and deep,
Where the tangles and the thickets
Make you want to go to sleep."

"We suggest you cycle southwards
Into meadows gay and bright,
Where the sunshine of fair Lincolnshire
May bring her into sight."

The cyclist crossed the Humber Bridge
On a day of wind and storm.
He questioned folk: "Where is she?"
But his hopes were quite forlorn.

They spoke in such confusion
That I have to paraphrase,
The gist was that they knew her
And she lived beside a maze!

He cycled on to Thornton Abbey
A labyrinth to find
Cut between the stalks of corn -
'Maize Maze" was the sign.

But no sign of Katrina
Met his hopeless gaze.
His cheeks so hollow, gaunt -
Might there be <u>another</u> maze?

A sudden smell of cooking
From a barbeque nearby,
Where people roasted corn cobs,
Sending smoke into the sky.

Sweet corn, sweet corn everywhere
Nor any cob to chew,
Sweet corn, sweet corn everywhere -
Of teeth he'd only two.

"Katrina does not live here,"
A passing seagull cried.
'Follow me to Alkborough!
Sorry, a long ride!"

The wheat was ripe and golden
In the rays of the setting sun.
"I hate you, lofty seagull!
I could shoot you with a gun.

"You're flying much too fast for me,
My legs are thin and weak."
But the gull flew on regardless
For he never heard him speak.

With streaks of red across the sky
The moon was rising, so late the hour,
The seagull landed dextrously,
The cyclist puffing, at Julian's Bower.

A medieval grassy maze
Of origin unknown,
A labyrinthine way to heaven,
Somewhat scruffy - and unmown.

And here upon a public bench
Donated by the gardener,
Sat in tears, in loud lament,
The elderly Katrina.

"Oh, where's my handsome cyclist,
So strong in limb, in thigh,
His teeth so white, so canine,
And that wondrous glittering eye?"

"I'm here, Katrina," the cyclist cried,
"I'd know you anywhere.
Though stouter round the middle,
The same glorious golden hair!"

"And you, my nameless cyclist,
Sans teeth, sans bulging thigh,
I'd pick you from a million
With your wondrous glittering eye."

The seagull left them hugging
On that bench by Julian's Bower.
They made up for many a lost year
Staying there hour upon hour.

Judging from the laughter, this one certainly capped them all. And unlike Chaucer (whose task was much more ambitious: two tales each, both to and from Canterbury), at least my Lincolnshire Tales ended up complete. To conclude, I will add a short quote which he was fond of using: *ther is namoore to tell.*

Epilogue - six months later

I never expected to be writing this, but here I am and still writing! Let me explain.

Every week Don drove me to see Jean in Winterton for healing. It was more than an hour's driving each way, so we would choose our favourite music to play in the car to help while away the time. It was hard work for him, poor lamb, but he never complained as he only wanted the best for me.

While Jean gave me healing, he would go to the Butchers Arms in the village for lunch, and gradually after a few weeks he became acquainted with some of the locals and enjoyed their conversation. On the way home he would share some of the village gossip with me so in a way those trips were good for us both.

Jean always said the same thing to me when I left. "Sit in the sun as much as possible, because you have no idea how beneficial and healing the sun's rays are. Simply absorb all those healing rays, and let nature take its course – who knows, you might even recover!"

So I would take out my deck chair as soon as the sun was shining, whether it was cold or warm, and I would simply lie back in it, exposing my head and arms and legs to the healing rays of the sun. Oh, and course, I only allowed hopeful positive thoughts to run through my mind, such as "I am getting better. In every way, I am gradually getting better." And I would have a smile for everyone who passed by (that is, if I wasn't dozing, which most of the time I was) and, following Jean's advice, I simply allowed nature to take its course.

One day we had a visit from David and his newly-discovered parents, Henry and Angela, who were now happily settled in Beverley. While the men went for a walk, Angela stayed with me and shared some of her memories of her time in Lincoln.

"It's such a relief to be away from there now," she said. "Once I was better after that appalling accident with David, I realised what a fool I'd been all those years ago, and yet it was too late to move as I didn't know anyone else so I was stuck with the place. But I gave up everything to do with books - I even stopped going to the cathedral - and went into catering. I'd always enjoyed cooking, so I started a little baking business, which was quite successful, and began supplying different cafés in the town."

"I suppose Henry told you all about that morning when we embarked on the search for you, enquiring in bookshops and gift shops," I said. "It seemed a lost cause at the time, but persistence was rewarded in the end."

"Henry told me it was the sight of those cakes in the reading café that set his saliva glands going. He confessed that if he hadn't been so greedy for Victoria Sponge, he might never have found me!"

"So now you're happily settled in Beverley?"

"I wouldn't say we're settled at all, because we spend all our time on holiday. We've already had a cruise in the Caribbean, and soon we'll be going on a railway journey across India. It's as though Henry is making up for lost time – he's so youthful and energetic and just sweeps me along with his enthusiasm. But I am happy to go along with it – so yes, to answer your question we're very settled and happy to be together again."

I was so pleased for them, and when the boys came back from their walk, I simply held my arms out from my beloved deck chair, and we all had a kind of deckchair embrace as well as we possibly could. It was wonderful to see them again, and looking so happy together.

But now I must complete the story about me, because the extraordinary thing is that I did recover from my dreadful illness. I would never have thought it possible, after the diagnosis I was given. But here I am, three months on, and feeling well enough to write these lines which I'd never expected to write, and able to bring this book to a conclusion.

So instead of coming for my funeral wake, my cycling friends are coming for a Christmas drink – and I believe one of them is intending to tell us about our next cycling adventure. How exciting is that!

How should I conclude this tale? Well, here's one way – my deck chair and I have been best friends for these last few months and I truly believe that if it hadn't been for its constant support while I absorbed the healing rays of the sun, I might never have recovered. So, in its honour, I wrote this rather silly ode, with which I shall conclude.

Ode to a Deck Chair, by Margot.

Striped object of much-vaunted bliss,
Your virtues are so hit and miss:
When folded up you're quiet and calm
But roused you can do serious harm -
Fingers pinched, tempers fray,
Is this your obtuse sense of play?
Confused we turn you inside out
While ugly oaths compelled to shout.
When finally we have you tamed,
The comfort for which you are so famed
Undoubtedly is the very best:
What luxury! Such easeful rest!
So why permit a nasty feature
To spoil things, you delightful creature?

The End